# NATURE AND OTHER MOTHERS

# NATURE
## AND OTHER
# MOTHERS

### REFLECTIONS ON THE
### FEMININE IN EVERYDAY LIFE

## BRENDA PETERSON

HarperCollins*Publishers*

Acknowledgments of sources follow page 216.

HarperCollins books may be purchased for educational, business, or sales promotional use. For information, please call or write: Special Markets Department, HarperCollins Publishers, Inc., 10 East 53rd Street, New York, NY 10022. Telephone: (212) 207-7528; Fax: (212) 207-7222.

FIRST EDITION

*Designed by Alma Hochhauser Orenstein*

Library of Congress Cataloging-in-Publication Data

Peterson, Brenda.
    Nature and other mothers: reflections on the feminine in everyday life / Brenda Peterson.
            p.        cm.
        ISBN 0-06-016313-5
        I. Title.
PS3566.E767N38  1992
814´ 54—dc20                                                    91-58374

92 93 94 95 96 MAC/HC 10 9 8 7 6 5 4 3 2 1

*for Beth, Susan, Paula, and Katherine*
*who each in her own way*
*has mothered this book*

# CONTENTS

# CONTENTS

## III
## WAR DIARIES

## IV
## NATURE AND OTHER MOTHERS

# ACKNOWLEDGMENTS

I would like to gratefully acknowledge my friend Joe Meeker for lending me the title from his original essay "Nature and Other Mothers," first written as a Mother's Day present for his wife, Maureen, and published in the journal *Between the Species* (Winter 1984). Deep thanks also to Flor Fernandez for her insightful support; to Louise Bode for listening; to Rebecca Lisa Romanelli for inspired play; to Linda Boudreau for wise nurturing; to my students for their heartfelt dialogue; to Rebecca Wells and her marvelous secretary, Merle, for an astute final editorial read, and to my editor, Hugh Van Dusen, for enthusiastically taking on this book. Finally, I would like to acknowledge my assistant, Beryl, a mad dog for details.

# PREFACE

Nature was my first mother—the fragrant, old forests of the Sierra Nevada mountains near the California-Oregon border, where my father worked on the Plumas National Forest. Living in a rough, small Forest Service cabin on vast acres of Douglas fir, mysterious blue spruce, and ponderosa pine, I memorized the forest floor as I would my mother's body. This forest skin smelled like pine sap and sweet rot that stained my diapers green and perfumed my hair, which was always tangled with bits of leaves, small sticks, and moss. It never occurred to me those early years on the forest that I was human. The small tribe of foresters and their families were not separate or, to a child's eyes, distinct from the forest.

The forest was my father's office; our log cabin belonged to my mother, much like a second skin of sideways timber. Because my mother was a town girl whom my father had wooed away from her wild, Wabash railroading ways; because my mother was a would-be writer who, in her own words, "had babies instead of books," I grew up with two strong sounds in my mind: my mother's typewriter tapping out words like the Morse code her fingers had once sent flying from her wartime electric telegraphy and waves of high-mountain wind through tall trees that had not yet been clear-cut.

Even after my mother's typewriter fell silent and many of the trees on my father's forest began to fall, the wilderness remained within me. I am imprinted by nature more deeply than I will ever make my own mark on this Earth. Because of that original body-bond, I long ago made a newborn's assumption that stays with me still: I am loved by nature, as I first loved her.

This is why at two, when I first left the forest to visit the Pacific Ocean, I simply opened my arms wide and ran straight into an undertow. She took me, as was her water way, and I tumbled over and over, tucking myself back into the recently abandoned womb-posture. There was no struggle—I remembered to breathe water. When the wave released me onto the sand, the only pain was air invading my chest again as my father pumped back my arms like wings on a baby bird whose wind is knocked out of its body after a fall from its forest nest. This drowning felt to me then like a second, distinct birth, with nature now as a vast body of water, as well as woods.

When I was four, we left the forest, "the field," as they call it in the government. Though my father spent the next thirty-seven years in the Forest Service, he was careful always to locate his family in country outside the city offices he disappeared into. With his successful career, we began our cross-country moves—zigzagging from California to New England, from Boston to Montana to Virginia, back to California, and then on to Georgia. If not for the fact that my parents are southerners with a strong, rooted tribe in the Ozarks and other southern strongholds; if not for the fact that my parents deposited us almost every summer at my grandfather's Ozark farm—we would have had no roots at all.

None of my younger siblings has ever lived any place longer than five years, in keeping with our transient childhoods. But ten years ago, when I first saw Puget Sound in Seattle, I felt again the physical recognition that I did with the forest and the ocean. Here I have stayed, near the water's wide and welcoming embrace.

The healing that comes from daily bonding with my recognized natural mother is also an apprenticeship to learning what the water, the animals, the forest can teach me. It is from them that I learn how to be more human.

I have also had other mothers who are still teaching me—siblings, friends, mates, and lovers, dolphins, whales, grandparents, parents, and aunts who show me how to midwife my own life.

This book explores many other teachers that can mother our minds, such as personal disarmament, or mourning ourselves and our Earth as a way of moving into more authentic ways of being. Playfulness and humor can teach us much about survival: the human body is also a compelling teacher, if we embrace it as wise; then there are the myriad daily rituals and chores, long the territory of the feminine, which can restore us to a sense of sacredness so often lost in modern society.

Halfway through my life, I offer these reflections as a record of the journey so far. These essays were written and lived over a decade, from 1982 to 1992. I hope they show not that I have arrived but that I am simply under way. As Carl Jung has written, "The encounter with the creature changes the creator." This creature, this book, is my own coming to terms with accepting that change, as well as a recognition of all the mothering minds, hearts, and hands that nurture it.

—BRENDA PETERSON
*Seattle, 1992*

*The Tao is called the Great Mother ...*
*It is always present within you.*
*You can use it any way you want.*

—LAO-TZU, *TAO TE CHING*
(STEPHEN MITCHELL TRANSLATION)

# I

# OTHER TEACHERS
# THAN TERROR

# OTHER TEACHERS THAN TERROR—FROM DINOSAURS TO DOLPHINS

W hen I was a child, my imaginary friends were dinosaurs. My favorite was Brontosaurus, whom I often found foraging in the basement near our fallout shelter for the fierce survivor weeds growing up through cracks in the foundation cement.

Those days I, too, was a little survivor looking for openings in my parents' southern fundamentalism, facing the terror of our Virginia hamlet's ground-zero neighbor, Washington, DC, and enduring our school's frequent civil defense drills.

Every time we ducked and covered—our teacher told us Russia had all its missiles aimed right at our hearts in the nation's capital, and I imagined when the bombs hit all our heads would explode in geysers of brilliant blood—I would call in my dinosaur troops. R. Tyranno would grab a bomb with those steel claws and hold it high until he could defuse it with his amazingly agile hands; Brontosaurus bent over me, a gentle bodyguard against shattering glass and flying desks or other children propelled midair like small, helpless human rockets; Ichthyosaur (Iki, I called her) would swim in the air alongside me, waiting for the still moment when right there in the hurricane eye of the end-of-the-world, she'd offer me her dorsal fin and speed off to safety. I'd grab my brother and sisters, and we'd all hang on for dear life as Iki leaped and dived and carried us back to the sea. Then we'd all leave this dangerous land that was on fire and go back into the ocean, where we were all still little enough to remember how to breathe underwater.

That was my own civil defense plan. And, when I compared it with what our teacher told us about emergency evacuation by bus and military personnel, or my mother's fervent explanations of the Biblical Rapture, when God would lift cars and trucks and churches up into the air for eternity, my plan seemed a lot more practical.

Over the years I kept my civil defense strategies to myself, just as I hid my dinosaurs. Mostly they lived in our basement, R. Tyranno's great tail wrapped around the Ping-Pong table, and Iki was out in the irrigation ditches running near our house. Brontosaurus holed up in the fallout shelter, but she was so big she filled the whole room with its shelves of canned food, distilled water, candles, the Bible, and a Monopoly game.

When I was in fifth grade, the world ended again for my dinosaurs. One day the teacher abruptly announced that we were all to go straight home—no duck-and-cover drill, just hide and hope the Russian missiles aiming at us from Cuba didn't seek. It was the late autumn of 1962, the week that would culminate in Black Saturday, when even our top leaders wondered if the world would see another morning. Schools dismissed, people set to stockpiling food and supplies, their fallout shelters fully operational. This was no test, the teacher said; this was real. "Go home, children," she'd said more softly than we ever imagined her voice could be.

We all stampeded home like animals fleeing before a forest fire—eyes wide and white. "What's happening? What's happening?" R. Tyranno and Bronto were nowhere to be found. Iki guided us home.

Mother met me at the door and sent all of us kids straight down to the fallout shelter. We hid, candles flickering as we listened to the transistor radio. President Kennedy's Yankee voice crackled and warned the Russians to withdraw their missiles from Cuba or face retaliation. I'd seen pictures of Cuba and Castro, a man who looked like a Neanderthal in a drab baseball cap smoking a cigar. I could believe that someone with a face like that might start a war.

Strangely calm, we all sat in our shelter's semidark, wondering if our father, with his top-security clearance, would stay in DC or come home to us. As I gazed around at my siblings, their faces ancient and familiar in the candle firelight like a tribe long before civilization, I felt so sad. They were too little to die. But I was not afraid, not until the moment I glanced up and at last saw my beautiful Brontosaurus. Curled around her great self, she was so terrified that basement weeds still hung from her mouth, uneaten.

Terror takes away hunger, I realized; there is a different kind of hunger, and that has to do with simply wanting, more than anything else in the world, to live. I recognized this other hunger in my Bronto's eyes—the biggest eyes I'd ever seen, dark and deep and afraid to die.

"There's ...," I began, not knowing I spoke aloud, "there's not enough room ..."

"No, no, we have plenty of air," my mother answered me, already somewhat panicky from her own claustrophobia.

But I wasn't speaking to her; I was talking to Bronto, who, coiled like a stricken leviathan, gazed at me with pity and fear and understanding. My sisters and brother all seemed as giddy and grim as my mother. They played Monopoly and ate three Whitman Samplers my mother had stashed for just such an emergency.

So there, during the Cuban missile crisis, I watched my sisters put hotels on Park Place and ruin my little brother's meager Oriental properties. I watched my mother fall into a drowsy trance, from either the chocolate or lack of oxygen. We would not last, I knew. I never had to ask my beloved Brontosaurus. Without a cry, without a protest, with only a tender gaze in her great eye, she let herself out of that fallout shelter and out of my world. She joined R. Tyranno and Iki and went to where everything extinct goes—maybe where we would go.

We stayed in that fallout shelter until late that night, when my father found us. For the rest of that week, we spent so much time in our shelter that we depleted our supplies; by Black Saturday we were cranky, hungry, sick of sweets, and ready to kill one another. I still have a pointed scar on my left wrist from my sister's thumbnail; she dug in astonishingly deep when I lucked out, didn't land on her row of low-class hotels, and instead went directly to jail.

The morning the Russians finally relented and we surprised ourselves by actually being happy to go to school, I walked through the woods, calling to my dinosaurs to come back. But they stayed gone so long that I at last realized they didn't *want* to come back and be here in the world with me. And for the first time I understood that there is a part of all of us that doesn't want to be here. Why else would we have decided to blow up our home and go extinct?

I have lived away from the East Coast now for over sixteen years and in that time told a few people about my imaginary friends who could save me during duck-and-cover drills but who died out during the Cuban missile crisis—the closest we've come in the postwar years to World War III. My room is full of dinosaur drawings, posters, prints. For birthdays friends have given me intricately sculpted or painted *Tyrannosaurus rex* and brontosaurus, and I have my own private set of dinosaur stamp pads and a Dino Alphabet.

I have not done a duck-and-cover drill since childhood. And now that the Cold War is officially over, how can I parlay all my childhood civil defense survival skills into another way of facing the world—not hunched over with the dread and terror of nuclear death, but a posture of openness and flexibility? So many years of being on "Red" alert have left many of us children of the Cold War like insomniacs afraid to dream the national nightmare. But as I begin to imagine a future without the simplistic morality play of Us and Them, I glimpse a spacious new storyline that does not presume extinction for my own or others' species.

One day last summer something happened that captured my imagination as if I were again a child. I was lounging on my backyard breakwater wall, staring at the high tide of Puget Sound, when suddenly a gigantic wave rose up and right over me. Out of nowhere it came, followed by three more waves so huge and fast I couldn't scramble away. Drenched and amazed, I looked for a sign of a barge or big freighter bound for Seattle's harbor through this sea-lane bordering my home. Nothing. All the neighbors ran out and stared. "What's happening! What's happening?" they cried.

My know-it-all neighbor on the left informed us all authoritatively that it was a submarine.

"No!" corrected the neighbor boy on the right with equal certainty. "It was a whale."

And then I started laughing, because here it was all over again: Big people believe anything bigger than they is destructive; and children, limited only in physical size, regard anything bigger as part of nature, and perhaps an imagined friend. To children, what's big is not necessarily bad; often their survival depends upon it.

The next morning, I woke up with one distinct question: If I have a choice when I die, where would I want to go?

I had been schooled in the sky God who will swoop us all away in a fiery flash as if it is righteous mercy and rescue to remove us from something so contaminated with sin as the Earth. Isn't the logical end of our contempt for the Earth to pollute and finally blow it up in fulfillment of the divine plan? Isn't nuclear holocaust simply an acting out of our own religious myth of judgment and retribution?

* * *

But that morning after the wave washed over me, I awoke and realized with absolutely certainty that if I had choice in the matter I'd elect to stay here on Earth, unlike my long-ago dinosaurs. In fact, I'd be very honored to reincarnate as a whale or dolphin.

And so began my cetacean education. I began whale watching in the San Juan Islands near Victoria, BC. There the Strait of Juan de Fuca is teeming with migrating gray whales, orcas, and dolphins. At Lime Kiln Point the orcas come right up to the rocks to scratch barnacles off their great backs. Summers sitting on those rocks, I saw the same scene played out between land mammals and sea mammals. Slack-faced, sated tourists all came alive when the whales breeched, breathing like thunder; then all ran to the very edge of the rocks, their hands—those tools of human technology whose delicate, fingered skeletons still exist inside cetacean pectoral fins, an evolutionary reminder of the land mammals who chose to return to the sea and spawn a parallel species—outstretched as if reaching for a lifeline. As these orcas (largest and fastest of the dolphin species) leapt high, scanning the crowds, actually making eye contact, people fell back in awe. Many wept without a trace of self-consciousness. Mostly there was a childlike joy, as if the whales restored us all to wonderment.

All summer my dreams swam with cetaceans, and finally one night I dreamt of a luminous white dolphin who beached herself purposefully to lie in my arms as I sat in the waves with her, midwifing four newborn. In my dream I saw what I later discovered with a shock of recognition in a textbook: dolphin and human fetuses are, eerily, anatomic mirror images. It was then I decided to write a children's book on whales and dolphins.

So last Christmas a friend and I traveled to a backwater lagoon in the Florida keys, and stared into the lucid, benevolent eye of a young male dolphin, until recently wild. He raised his long, slender head to gaze at me intently while I stroked that sensuous, cool, and elegant bottle nose. He emitted those by now familiar, almost-out-of-register creaks and whistles, all the while floating sideways, the better to study me. He never once broke eye contact, and I remembered my marine biologist friend telling me that dolphins are the only other species who use eye contact as a major form of social interaction. In or out of water, dolphins' eyes are much more penetrating than ours. Anyone who has ever returned a dolphin's deep gaze—and the literature, both scientific and more fanciful, is replete with accounts of feeling completely well met by these fellow creatures—will report the sense of communion and profound contact with another mind, a presence. There is no fear.

In the blazing December sun, my three companions and I sat listening to the research marine biologist at the research center school us in dolphin etiquette. We sat on small benches with our snorkels, flippers, and life preservers, listening closely while all around us bobbed the dolphins who were to be our escorts as we entered their watery world. Gone was the distance of observer and observed in zoos or captive tanks. Here we were in *their* element at last, and I can only say I felt a graciousness and welcoming curiosity on the part of the dolphins as they awaited our swim.

All inferior status as pets or performers was gone now

that it was we humans who were willingly being used as dolphin playmates. The marine biologists were not studying how well dolphins adapt to humans; they were watching to see what the dolphins might make of us.

"Remember," said our researcher, "there is nothing more boring to a dolphin than a human bobbing around, mouth agape, staring. If you want to play with the dolphins, you'll have to offer them some creative alternative to their own sporting about."

She went on to teach us carefully about first contact. There were four humans, two dolphins in our lagoon: my friend and I and two teenage boys, neither of whom had lost his cool, though they did betray some excitement. Individually we entered the seawater, which was surprisingly warm, sweet smelling. As I'd been taught, I held out my hands, palms facing the dolphins, who in a flash passed me by as I stroked them, smooth nose to graceful tail. It was so quick, this touch, more like a wing or wave lap. Yet in that instant each dolphin had astutely scanned me.

There is no hiding from dolphins. Their extraordinary powers of perception include echolocation, a sonar that doesn't stop at the skin but, like ultrasound, "sees" the exact state of our insides. Their acoustic holograms show them our emotions and our health. By the tumult of gases in our intestines, say, the dolphins decipher if we are afraid, angry, sad. Imagine a perception that penetrates all appearances. Researchers have noted again and again that cetaceans respond most to our emotional life, reading it as well as they do. There are other studies on possible telepathic communication among dolphins—perhaps they send images one to another. It seems doubtful that we will ever catch up to the cetaceans' keen sense of hearing. Their evolution lost the sense of smell but so heightened visual, kinesthetic, and acoustic skills that we, their land family, can only marvel. To hear our voices, a dolphin must tune down its frequency, the vibration of its sound waves, to the lowest decibel, or the skills of a newborn dolphin.

No wonder I found myself whistling, singing underwater, and trying to imitate that high, rapid-fire whine of dolphin language, like the high-frequency tone of a jet engine just gearing up for takeoff. Fortunately, the researcher had planned a few interactions by way of acquainting us with our dolphin escorts. At the sound of a whistle way out of our register, the dolphins came to each of us and presented their pectoral fins for a dance. I was lifted out of the water several feet by my dolphin, an older female, who again made eye contact as we danced; then she gently dropped me, clicked rapidly, and streaked away.

I have never been lifted up by anything not human— except my long-ago imaginary friends. And in that moment a generosity I had only imagined became so real I began shivering, not from fear, from happiness. I had read that the French are experimenting with dolphins as a treatment for depression. I understood why when I was tenderly lifted up, danced around, then delicately let go by my dolphin mate. It was not a mothering, it was the play of peers, with extra care taken on the part of the mammal most adept at zero gravity.

Imagine a world without weight or struggle, an element through which one's body floats, spirals, and dives in watery flight. Muscles and skin are streamlined, hydrodynamically in perfect sync with their environment. Perhaps in such a sea there is no need for that manipulative hand to conquer or replace or re-create a competitive environment. Where we might construct a bridge, a book, a pair of shoes, the cetaceans might create a memory and language so vast it can hold all they have ever learned about their world, themselves.

There is something else to consider, a scientific fact that is simple but provocative. Cetaceans have another brain not found in humans; called the paralimbic lobe, this feature of the cerebral cortex synthesizes all senses. Our sense receptors are scattered over various regions of our brain. This scattering is the effect of an evolution based on a heightened response to danger. For example, if one hears an unexpected loud noise, the sense of hearing does not have to wait to be integrated with other senses before the brain can respond. One can simply act in self-defense. But this skill can limit us, because our neural functions can become isolated one from another. What if that loud noise is not a threat but a delight? A bass drum in an unexpected parade, a welcoming call of a whale, a gunshot signaling celebration? We might have fled or defended ourselves needlessly. With our senses so separated, we can act without a grasp of the whole picture.

Imagine experiencing the world with all senses integrated into the whole; this is hologrammatic intelligence. And I believe this is what we may now have to learn to survive in the future. Not the eye-hand, manipulative skills of technological conquest but the synthetic, holistic mind that whales might lend us if only we could assent to be apprenticed to another species.

As we swam freely in that humid Florida lagoon, our

dolphin guides deftly maneuvering their sleek, 400-pound bodies under our arms for momentary rides, then dazzling us with leaps directly overhead, I gave way to a primitive playfulness, an abandon I certainly never knew in childhood. I had only imagined this freedom of play; I had only dreamed of Iki offering me her dorsal fin as one of the Florida dolphins did now. Holding on for dear life, laughing so hard I swallowed great gulps of salt water, I streaked through the water at what seemed the speed of light. Then the dolphins disappeared to dive with the teenage snorkelers, propelling them into the depths, from which they shot up, yelling in their adolescent lingo "Awesome!" Then they dove again, grabbing a dorsal.

With so much frolicking and high spirits, we forgot that we were land creatures and cavorted in gravity-defying leaps ourselves. I glanced over to the other lagoon and saw the British dowager who earlier had confessed anxiety singing at the top of her voice as an elder dolphin carried her aloft. (Later this crusty Brit told me the dolphins found the steel pin in her knee, which clicked with each bend, most communicative. One dolphin kept nudging her knee, excited that at last someone was attempting their language.)

In that hour, everywhere I turned the dolphins were with me. I'd spin, they'd spin. I'd sing, they'd click, clatter, and ratchet, nodding their glossy snouts. Every time I held out my hands, they'd slide by, the intimate, powerful *twoooosh* of their black, puckered blowholes shushing me. Dolphins exhale at the velocity of 100 miles per hour. But what I will never forget is their skin. Twenty times more tactile than ours, the dolphins' skin feels fast, silken, sensitive as quicksilver.

At last they tendered their final act of grace. Without a sound, in perfect sync, both dolphins shot up on either side of me, offering their dorsal fins. Each waited in harmony until I had hold, then we were off. To fly through air and sea with dolphins as my wings, to be borne along between those two beings who are in equipoise with their element and themselves—forget gazing at the sky for our only signs of the divine, or the star people who will somehow rescue us from our wayward world, Heaven is *here* and humbly offering its peace on Earth—that's what I thought as the dolphins smoothly carried me to shore.

As I watched both dolphins return for my friend, who took her turn treading water, arms outflung at her sides, it struck me that this opening wide of one's arms and waiting to be carried aloft is our Western symbol for the rapture of crucifixion—Christ on the cross, arms wide, offering his body in tragic transcendence.

Though our gesture of opening to those dolphins was the same, there was no hint of tragedy. It was high comedy, a happy ending, a marriage of true minds. Finally, as I watched my friend streak toward shore between those dolphins, mouth stretched wide in a smile full of seawater, I understood why as a child I had chosen not R. Tyranno or Bronto but Ichthyosaur to carry me to safety.

Tragedy cannot carry us. It may inspire, provoke pity and terror and a certain self-knowledge. But tragedy is intricately bound to the past, not the future. It teaches and tells us what is moral and good, but it does not celebrate life or survival. In fact, it deifies death. It is the comic traditions that carry on life, however haphazard and unnoble. It is the holy fools, the playful who imagine that life is preferable.

Say a man is committing suicide because he has failed himself or those he loves; say he's killed or followed his fate and offended the gods. Say this man decides to walk into the sea and sink into forgetfulness, righteous self-judgment. Say this man is besieged by sharks even as his mythologizers begin the stories that will transform his act into a tragic tale by which we, the hearers, are supposed to live better. If there are dolphins nearby, they will circle this man and offer their fins, no matter how much he flails in holy terror and the human passion play of self-sacrifice. The dolphins will simply wait until the man is unconscious—all passion spent—before hooking his out-flung arms over their dorsal fins and floating him gently to beach with the living.

When a dolphin dies, it is often carried like this in a high seas ceremony before sinking to rejoin the food chain, that great salt sea change. And whale cows will often carry a dead calf for days, until it disintegrates. What does this say about the cetacean clinging to life, carrying it along even after the life force has left? I think it says something about honoring life more than death, about being more responsible to life than to glorification of an afterlife. I think it celebrates the beauty and harmony of the Earth not as holier than the sky but simply as in balance with the heavens.

When our time with the dolphins was up, I was the last to leave the lagoon. I knelt by the turquoise salt water, its tide high, and again gazed into the steady eye of that young dolphin. Again the high, piercing whistles and clacks, the whirring just out of my ear's reach. Here was reunion, I thought, not only with Iki, whom I believed lost, but with a part of myself. And it was with complete calm that I also acknowledged something I could not have admitted before my dolphin swim: It was I, not the enemy Russians or Neanderthal Castro, who had long ago killed my imaginary friends. Granted, it was a child's response to the threat of war and a decision to act for my own survival. Nevertheless, it was I who had willed my dinosaurs to leave the world. Perhaps subconsciously I had never believed the world safe enough to summon them back.

My culpability, some thirty years after the fact, did not come with despair. Instead I felt the calm truth of it, along with a bone-deep sense of my own responsibility and the paradox of creativity. Those who are the most creative are also the most destructive. Because we humans create things outside ourselves, we must also destroy, if only to re-create something else again in their place, perhaps the future. The skills of the murderer are also the skills of a visionary: the ability to perceive a life without that which one must destroy, the relentlessness to rid oneself of what is in one's way, be it a bad habit or a survival tool that has long outgrown its usefulness.

Post–Cold War our tragic tradition, evident now in our reaching the Balance point of perfect technological empathy—I push the button and I, too, die—must give way so that we might imagine another future. If the mind blanks at nuclear war, the creators among us must take the responsibility to destroy within ourselves (*not* as projected onto an imaginary enemy) those outmoded survival strategies that worked when we were still just tool-wielding and danger-dodging. It is not now a question of surviving our enemy; it is a question of surviving ourselves. We cannot turn outward for this next stage of our evolution; we must turn inward. And it is in that inner world that the cetaceans have so long waited for us to join their journey.

If we take responsibility for the world we have made and don't allow ourselves the option of a tragic end, i.e., death (which is, after all, an escape from taking responsibility in this world), then we might be able to imagine our species sticking around long enough to evolve other ways of living. Think of a hand that over aeons evolves into a fin for efficient navigating in a sea where hands are obsolete. Think of a mind that shapes itself in response to the need for communication, emotional development, affection, play, and memory of all that has gone before. Think of a survival strategy based on a divinity implicit in life more than death, in the earth more than the sky, in the comic tradition of coming together.

Think once more of a human tribe in which there is no bomb out there threatening us but instead each individual has his or her own weapon: the ability to stun and so disorient one's prey. One of the current fascinations among marine biologists is studying a cetacean community wherein everyone is a weapon. How do they balance aggression? The dolphins have in their sophisticated echolocation the ability to stun a fish or predator by emitting high-voltage sound waves. This is a balance of power that humans have just now arrived at in creating nuclear parity.

Our nuclear arsenals now equal 250 tons of TNT for every man, woman, and child in the world. If we accept that at some level each human being carries his or her own bomb, we arrive at the dolphin tribal deterrence. Why are there no dolphin wars? Why has there been no recorded incident of a dolphin ever harming a human, its fellow mammal? Why do dolphins, in fact, rescue us even as a tuna-fishing industry, in defiance of our Marine Mammal Protection Act, destroys on the average of 300 dolphins a day worldwide?

Perhaps the answer lies in the way dolphins deal with violence among themselves. If a young dolphin is too aggressive, his mother will forcibly butt him to teach him proper tribal boundaries. If the aggression continues, the mother and perhaps an elder dolphin will evoke the most dreaded experience—they will, by holding the young dolphin underwater, suggest drowning. Death by drowning is always a risk for a dolphin or whale. When they rest on the waves, there are always sentinels alert to gently hoist or lift a fellow creature up for air if its rest borders too near unconsciousness. If a cetacean is knocked unconscious, it will drown. So this breathless reprimand is usually enough to deter aggression within the tribe. But should that aggression persist, and in rare cases it does, the dolphin tribe will simply and absolutely shut out that individual. They will not respond to his sonar cries, his frequencies; though he swims alongside them, they will not acknowledge his existence. The exiled dolphin will languish behind his tribe, utterly dejected, will stop feeding, though the fish be all around him, and will finally die of loneliness and abandonment. The dolphin's intense need for affection and a highly developed emotional life is the survival tool that has determined his species' evolution.

Humans, by contrast, have often selected the most aggressive individuals and chosen an intelligence that favors strategic thinking, defense of the group, and goal-oriented communication. We have learned to increase our brain size in response to the stimulus of stress and survival of the fittest. It is no coincidence that here on the brink of a new, more conscious form of evolution, we must consider that stress itself has become our most insidious health hazard. Stress—once our evolutionary trigger—is now our killer. It is a survival tool well on its way to assuring our extinction.

The common theory these days about the disappearance of dinosaurs is that of catastrophe, the violent end of a species. If this theory holds true, my childhood intuition of losing my own dinosaurs to what I thought was nuclear war was sadly true. If catastrophe causes extinction, then any struggle for military superiority at this dangerous stage is a form of natural selection that will one day inevitably select against us.

What other teachers do we have than terror, intimidation, and physical force? We've been so apprenticed to the sky God's thunderbolts, we've forgotten the lessons of this Earth and her creatures.

Long ago, when the gods were also animals, shamans and storytellers asked the Great Bear, the whales and dolphins, the birds and snakes and night creatures to come to them as messengers from the gods, as teachers, as guides. In these tribal societies, before science explained everything, a woman might find herself pregnant by the spirit of the jaguar or the cobra. Upon her giving birth, that child would forever be kin to his or her animal progenitor.

I have at last reunited with my fellow creatures. Dolphins—named from the Greek *delphe,* or "womb," those creatures once worshiped as gods, as guides to carry the soul to the underworld, long-ago totems of Aphrodite as mistress of the sea, as keeper of the sacred breath of life and symbol of rebirth, dolphins as the smallest and most accessible of whales—these are the guides I've asked to be with me this time round.

Perhaps if we could acknowledge the life-denying bomb within each of us, as well as reunite with our own Earth and her animals, we might learn to defuse ourselves. We might then also evolve from murderers to visionaries. Finally, we might do much more than simply survive; we might have some fun doing it and develop a comic tradition that loves life.

I no longer have imaginary friends who die out. I can look to my dolphins and the whales. Physicists theorize that, by the simple act of observing something outside ourselves, we change that object. But I have not felt changed by the dolphins' deep and perceptive intelligence. I've simply felt seen. In the South, they call it "witnessing." When we witness one another, when we open ourselves to allow another species to observe us as well, there is much healing in the humility.

And there is something else—companionship. In exchanging a clear, steady gaze with another species, we are reminded that we are not here alone.

# VASTER THAN EMPIRES
# AND MORE SLOW

Some midnight, midcontinent, streaking across Kansas in a honeymoon sleeper, my parents made me. My mother had recently retired at age twenty-one from her wartime years as a station telegrapher on the Wabash "Cannonball" line. In the toss-up between her railroading and marriage to a young forester, my father won. But not for long.

Though he took my mother away from her first steamy, steel love, he couldn't take trains from her blood. Riding the rails runs in our family like a dominant gene. Some families pass along sharpshooter eyes or stolid legs like roots—but my sisters and brother and I inherited a hobo waywardness.

In fact, our uncle *was* a hobo. Our earliest stories of my mother's brother, Clark, were of dropping him at a railroad crossing in the middle of a California desert. He knelt by the tracks as if in prayer. After a long while he leapt up, slung his knapsack and bedroll over his shoulder, and sprinted off. But where was the train? Uncle Clark counted aloud as he ran, shouting with what we children instantly recognized—though it was rare in adults—as sheer joy.

Suddenly the ground thundered, and, as if called, a train caught up with Uncle Clark. It slowed only a little, but not enough to be caught, even by my uncle, strong and sleek as he was. Undaunted, Uncle Clark let out a piercing whistle. Out of the black square shadow of one boxcar shot a long arm. In a flash my uncle grabbed it and was hoisted inside the wide door. We never saw the other hobo, we only heard them laughing at the show they'd given us townies.

Not too long after that, our parents yielded to their four children's clamor to take a cross-country train ride from California to St. Louis for the usual summer stint with our Ozarkian kin. The first night in our drawing room, my three-year-old sister frog-kicked my father out of the top berth and knocked Mother silly. Unperturbed by the hubbub above, my other sister, baby brother, and I played Parcheesi in the bottom berth. I remember most the horizons that gently curved both Earth and steel tracks as we rolled along. The world was wide and open— and so were we. We even endured my father's lectures on the changing flora and fauna.

"This used to be buffalo country," he'd say sadly as empty Midwest prairie swept by. We imagined shaggy ghosts grazing in the sweet grass. Sometimes Father would quiz us as if it weren't summer vacation at all. "Did you know, kids, that ninety-nine percent of this country's population lives on one percent of the land?"

Cities seemed so silly to us when we saw the vast green

thrust of corn, the cows who kept chewing their cuds even as this iron leviathan shrieked alongside them. Such spaciousness, we decided, makes daydreamers of animals and people. We stared out the window at the cows, chewing our bubble gum, our eyes half-lidded. We'd even forget to blow bubbles. After all, our so-called Vista-Dome was already a cool, blue bubble.

Our family still takes trains cross-continent, in this era of faxes and flight. Trains are a trance state that makes planes seem high-pitched, a hysteria. The human heart is slow. How, in the space of several hours, can we really adjust to opposing sides of a continent? How comprehend leave-taking, longing, loss, or even love?

Uncle Clark, who is now retired from Social Security, still vacations near narrow-gauge railroads, and many Sundays he reads the paper down at the local depot, counting trains and chatting with ex-Cannonball conductors. My sister Paula, her three girls, and I now consider the Silver Meteor line, which runs up and down the eastern seaboard from Miami to New York City, as our home away from home.

On these trips we've tallied up one madman, one car hit by our train, and one fatal heart attack. Because my sister is a surgical nurse, we're often in on the action. The cigar-smoking madman we named Mr. Neanderthal. He screamed at the conductor loud enough to make him turn over our sleeper to him because Amtrak had double-booked it; then Mr. Neanderthal barricaded himself inside. We rode most of the twenty-two hours in the dining car, with free wine and stories from the stewards. They reported that Mr. Neanderthal was in our ex-sleeper, clad in nothing but his skivvies, with a gun in one hand and an egg salad sandwich—presumably packed by Mrs. Neanderthal—in the other. He was threatening to buy Amtrak because he was so rich and so angry.

It was during the heart attack—the man was past help from Paula's CPR—that a conductor informed us, "No one ever dies on a train. They always die in the nearest city." He told us the story of an old couple traveling from Miami to Hoboken, New Jersey. For hours the stewards eyed this man, who never moved or spoke, his hat crunched down over his face. Yet his food disappeared, and his wife chatted with him. "But, you know, that guy was awful still," the conductor said. "Finally I approached the couple and said, 'Ma'am, is your husband all right?' She waved me off and said, 'He's *always* been quiet.'

"Well"—the conductor laughed—"that old guy wasn't quiet; he was dead. But when we tried to insist upon moving him and stopping the train so we could call the ambulance, his wife screamed bloody murder. Then she pleaded with me, 'Can't you just carry my husband on to Hoboken in baggage?'"

This past summer, Paula planned her greatest train trip to date—traveling from West Palm Beach cross-country to San Francisco, then up to Seattle, along the Canadian border, then back down to Florida. When my family heard about my sister's train adventure, we all signed up to join her on various jogs. Mother boarded and rode from DC to Philadelphia; and I flew to San Francisco to take the Coast Starlight train back to Seattle.

When I met my sister, her three girls, and their Colombian nanny in San Francisco, they had accumulated another friend, Madelyn, with her eight-year-old son and nineteen bags. "It's like traveling with the shah of Iran," I complained, as porters boarded us. We had booked two sleeper compartments in the same car. Over the next twenty-two hours we stretched ourselves, amoe-balike, between observation car, dining car, and compartments.

As the Coast Starlight steamed out of the Bay Area, we cozily settled ourselves into the dining car. "Our sleeper car is a regular soap opera," Paula happily reported. "See that couple over there? They've been riding since Atlanta—and the honeymoon is definitely over!"

"What is it about trains that makes ordinary people into the cast of 'As the World Turns'?" I asked.

"It's the close quarters," my sister explained. "Over the days everyone becomes a kind of gypsy family living in one long house."

She went on to fill us in on the details of our traveling companions. There was a Swiss family whose son had attached himself to our troop because his parents were preoccupied with a murderous, never-ending Monopoly game. Then there was the old lady in Sleeper C of our car who monopolized our steward because she believed first-class meant servants. Later I visited this intriguing, if demanding woman and heard her tales of having survived both the 1906 and the 1989 San Francisco earthquake. Seems railroading was in her blood, too. Her father was a conductor from Sparks, Nevada. Once he'd worked the legendary Olympian Hiawatha train, which once ran from Chicago to Seattle.

That first night the dining car was divine. As the adults lingered over elegant wine and peach pie, we sent the kids sprawling into the Vista-Dome, where they watched the movie *The Bear* on a big-screen TV. My nieces counted shooting stars like so many sparks thrown from the train. When we all finally retired to our tidy bunks, we were experts at the polite, lurching sidestep and shuffle of narrow aisles. Looking into each roomette as we slowly passed, I saw a man leaning over his needlepoint, an old couple nodding on each other's shoulders as they held hands, fast asleep; I peeked into another sleeper and eyed an entire family with attention riveted on their bleeping Game Boys and a teenage couple who might as well have been in the backseat at the drive-in. So much life right alongside mine.

As we all bunked down for the rockabye night, I figured we were somewhere lost between redwoods and northern California seacoast—wild land with only a few lights here and there. But inside this train was an intimacy, a tenderness as simple as sharing sleep. In our room's four bunks, we all hooked ourselves up to various headsets—everything from country and western to my own *Les Misérables* tape and my niece's "Sesame Street" songs. Lying happily in my berth, I gazed out the window at mountains silhouetted by a slight moon and gloried in the knowledge that this was how I chose to enter the world—by train.

Next morning during a breakfast of buttermilk hotcakes and sausage, we stared down chasms over coffee and hardly blinked as ancient Oregon forests surrounded us. Fog swirled as if the land were still asleep. We were at 5,000 feet outside Chemult, Oregon, when the mists cleared to reveal a mysterious, deep Odell Lake. The conductor told us in his leisurely travelogue that it is 300 feet deep. Staring down from the scant tracks we made as the Coast Starlight streaked across water, my niece insisted, "No, it's lots deeper. Something else lives there"—she looked at us, her expression at once wide-eyed and wise—"and it's not like us."

"Ohhhh, I don't know," my sister told her. "After a month on a train, what else *is* like us?"

She was right. I knew it, even after my mere sixteen-some hours. We were all changed. It wasn't the travel; it was the movement. Maybe it was the stirring in our genes, our blood—all my mother's mesmerizing miles, all my uncle's hobo longings, all our own accumulated memories of just rocking along going somewhere, but not fast.

The way we travel reveals the way we live. I like delayed gratification; I like a lingering hand, a lulling voice, a close and deliberate dance. "As slow as molasses in January," that's how my mother has always described taking trains. "Slow and sweet."

Already my sister and I are planning next summer's train trip. We rack up cross-country conference calls discussing the pros and cons of the Zephyr versus the Empire Builder. All winter we'll sort out which novels, clothes, games, and companions are just right for "the slow-motion adventure," as Paula calls our train rides. "Sometimes ...," she muses, as we talk long distance, "I think it takes almost as long to pack for a train trip as it does to take one."

We both laugh leisurely and fall silent. We've forgotten that there's a phone meter ticking away, we've forgotten all about expensive airwaves and the blank heavens above. We're thinking about buffalo ghosts in Kansas and a lake so deep there's nothing human about it. We might as well be lounging on our berths while something as slow and vast as a country drifts by us. Even cross-continent, we're on the same track, remembering all the sleepers that carried us, the steel that still vibrates in our blood, the great body that cradles us with long curves, with tunnels dark as dreams, with an unbroken embrace of Earth.

# IN PRAISE OF SKIN

*For R.L.R.*

In the snowy Seattle winter of 1985, after a month of high fevers and strep throat, I sat amid the holiday hubbub of our Thanksgiving table and noticed my hands and arms were breaking out in spots. By the time we were drinking our hot toddies before the fire, there were spots between my toes, lightly marching across my face, up and down my legs.

In the course of the next week I was given three diagnoses. The emergency room declared my spots an allergy to antibiotics, my doctor suggested *psi roseola* or *guttate psoriasis,* and southern friends recognized it surely as "fever rash," a children's disease. For the next months I went around looking like a thirty-five-year-old woman with chicken pox. Incurable, they said; it'll come and go. My doctor called in an "unlimited" prescription for cortisone cream. At night my housemate played dot-to-dot, dabbing the expensive cream on my back. Slowly the spots faded, only to return when I drank coffee, played racquetball. Stress-related, someone suggested. Maybe I was allergic to my own adrenaline?

I called my sister, a surgical nurse and mother of three girls. "I'm trying to imagine how you look with all those spots," she said. "Is it like when you sat on that wasps' nest at Grandad and Vergie's and got stung all over? Remember Vergie's cure?"

Of course I remembered—screaming in the front yard with welts swelling everywhere while my grandfather spat tobacco juice as a poultice until Vergie swooped me up in her arms and carried me to the metal tub in her farmhouse kitchen. Even in Vergie's arms, deep in the cool comfrey bath, my body felt flensed, too raw to touch. Yet Vergie kept running her hands all over, lightly cooing, shushing, talking to my skin as if tenderly telling it that now was a safe time to come back.

Then this stepgrandmother, who for many years had followed her beauty shop clients from her Cut 'n' Curl pink swivel chairs to the steel tables of the local morgue, where she moonlighted as a beautician, confided in me a secret ritual of her "beautification practice," as she called it. "Your body's skin," Vergie said, "is bigger, harder-working, and more wide open than the human heart; it's a sad thing to see how skin gets passed right over, barely touched except in sex, or sickness, or deep trouble. Why, we pay so little mind to our own skin, we might as well be living inside a foreign country."

Then she told me another secret. She considered it an honor and a sacred death chore to touch every inch of skin on a body before it was buried, just the way she was touching me now in my healing bath.

The beautification idea had come to Vergie when

Edna Crow died. Edna had just called to schedule a set and blue rinse, but Vergie met her in the morgue for their appointment. She'd long ago memorized Edna's head from many scalp massages during shampoos. And between the foot washings and laying-on-of-hands in church, the midwifing strokes and massages during Edna's three long labors, there was hardly a bit of Edna's body that Vergie didn't already know.

She also knew that Edna, widowed for decades, hadn't been touched in the simple, self-less petting that, as Vergie points out, "babies and even barnyard cats get." So it was Mrs. Crow in the stillness of the mortuary who received Vergie's first beautification practice. Lightly, with dignity and recognition, Vergie ran her hands along those old limbs, touched each worn fingertip, held that big toe that was once broken by a runaway grocery cart, and finally cupped that familiar head in her palms like a favorite bowl.

That day in Vergie's tub as she told me her secrets and stories, my skin healed so deeply that all the wasp sting spots were gone by morning.

"Yes," I told my sister, staring at my own hands again covered with spots. "I remember Vergie's cures."

"Well," my sister suggested softly, "Vergie would say you need some simple mothering." She laughed. "You need a good rubdown, baby." Thus I began a regimen of cool comfrey baths alternating with hot eucalyptus rubs.

All my life I'd followed Vergie's hands-on tradition by massaging the heads and feet of my family and friends. Now I set up a series of trades with two massage therapist friends: I worked on their heads and they on my skin. We tried everything that winter, but my mysterious spots would vanish and then reappear with their own logic. Then someone suggested that along with the baths and massage, I alternate racquetball with a more meditative exercise; why not try yoga, long known as a way of cleansing the body?

So one icy January evening my friend Gregory Bolton, a massage instructor at Seattle Massage School, and I attended our first yoga class. As I practiced the postures I felt my aching, raw skin expand, stretch, then release with my muscles—almost as if the skin itself were breathing.

My first yoga teacher, Rebecca Romanelli, a deep-tissue therapist, told me about the fourth chakra of the heart, traditionally associated with the sense of touch. "Skin is the body's biggest organ," she reminded me. "It breathes, filters, and protects. It's more important than the heart. Someone with a third of his heart blocked can still live and breathe—but if a body loses a third of its skin, it dies."

That spring, as the spots faded from my face, I began to study the *skin of things:* cool green watermelon rinds, the graceful flap of cornstalks and silks; green, cupped palms of cabbage heads, red chrysalides of ripe tomatoes; the scarlet peel of pomegranate, symbol of immortality or— for Persephone—a season in the underworld. I found myself studying animal skin, running my hands along the tanned, soft hides that were our species' first mythical and physical survival—to hide inside the body of a greater animal, for warmth, for camouflage, to borrow spiritual power.

One summer night during another bout with fever and spots, I had a dream. All around me stood ancient

Chinese doctors, men and women, their faces fragile as rice paper, skin luminous as the translucent surface of water when the sun shines on it just so. They were laughing and running their hands up and down my body. I recognized Vergie among them; then I relaxed, resting as they smiled and raised their robed arms. On their sleeves were brilliant symbols and moving pictographs. All the while they ran those beautiful, tapered hands up and down my body, I lay beneath them, laughing. When I awoke my fever had broken and my spots were almost completely gone.

Perhaps it was the laughter—something I'd been in short supply of that year-of-the-spots. I remember that morning after my dream as one might a hallucination. All my senses heightened, I ran my hands along my clear belly, my arms and legs, my at last unblemished brow. I felt a radiant well-being, as if I'd grown new skin in the night. It was the way a snake must feel when it finally slithers free from what it once believed it could not live without, only to find a glowing, new expanse of skin.

Over the next years I continued yoga and massage work; learning to be at home in my own body, and sensually more at home with other bodies, be they male or female companions. But not until recently did I come to realize that the Chinese-doctor dream had to do with larger healing. Another friend, Bettelinn Krizek Brown, who has practiced massage and yoga for over eighteen years, introduced me to a ritual that reunites me with Vergie's hands-on tradition.

Called *jin shin jytsu* or "the art of compassionate being," this ancient Oriental healing art was originally practiced not by doctors but in the home. Long ago in China the *jin shin* laying on of hands was anchored to oral formulas, stories that have since been lost. But the physical practice was rediscovered by Master Jiro Murai of Japan, who in turn taught it to Mary Ino Burmeister, who brought it to this country. My own teacher, Betsy Dayton, founder of the High Touch Network in Friday Harbor, Washington, studied with Burmeister and has had her own practice for fourteen years.

*Jin shin* is a *yin* or feminine approach to the hands-on healing tradition. Like acupuncture, the art follows the ancient Oriental meridians of energy in the body; but since *jin shin* uses only the deep, electromagnetic energy of the human hands, it is not intrusive like the *yang* or masculine, projectile approach of needles. It is also feminine in that there is no exchange of energy, but more a support for the body to tap into its own energy and unblock the various pressure points. Fluid and subtle, yet powerful, the acupressure treatments are called "flows" and the *jin shin* hands learn to see and listen to the body's pulses.

In *jin shin*, the skin symbolizes a level of energy cycling associated with the lung and large intestine, the element of metal, the color white, the sound of weeping, the season of autumn, the very early morning, and the emotion of grief. According to these ancients, grief is the first emotion one must learn, the moment one recognizes his or her own separate skin. But this experience can lead to a physical epiphany. Skin need not be some earthly prison—it is the way a soul may choose to experience, to feel, and finally to embody what on a spiritual level one might already know. And perhaps this is what it is to be human: to reach out for warmth, for light, for another skin with the part of oneself that is the most tangible, the most vulnerable, the most mortal.

Finally, every inch of skin's embrace is a self-regulating, self-healing system. Recent medical research supports this more intuitive understanding in its discovery that skin plays a previously unsuspected and crucial role in maintaining the body's biochemistry, and that the skin's role in producing interferons is vital to a healthy immune system.

It is sad and curious that our biggest health fear, an epidemic of AIDS, has to do not with a plaguelike virus or inner misfiring of cells like cancer but a breaking of skin. We have upon us a disease that redefines lovemaking from strictly intercourse to two bodies simply being together. We are in a sexual age that throws us back on touch. Touching one another in that abiding ritual distinct from sex is something Victorians knew all about. But we moderns have much to learn or, as the Chinese doctors reminded me, to remember.

Our sexual revolution's anchor of skin and touch strictly to sex is an impoverishment deeper than any repressive century before us. Amid our society's expanse of exposed skin, the flaunt of flesh, we are not really touched, known, memorized in what was Vergie's tradition. In fact, many of my massage therapist friends tell me they know more about their clients' bodies than their husbands or wives or lovers. "A shame," Vergie would say, "a crying shame." And it's the hands that are crying.

When I'm working with my hands these days, I think

of Vergie. She is the only person I know who if blinded could recognize an old lover, her husband, her children, her stepfamily, and all her clients by hand.

Perhaps it will take us all our lives to fully possess our own and recognize others' skin. In doing so, we might well practice in Vergie's hands-on tradition: a deep attention to skin that is a healing art, that abides with the body and has no expectations, no goals—not lovemaking, not changing, not correcting this or that muscle or bone, but just *being with* another's body, memorizing its pulses and curves and hollows as if hands could hear and see and somehow let be, even while embracing.

# QUEEN OF CUPS

**W**hen my agent called with the good news, I was slightly horrified. "*Cosmopolitan* wants my story? I can't believe it."

"Fingers crossed." My agent murmured the words like an incantation. "All the other *Cosmo* editors love it, now let's see what Helen Gurley Brown has to say."

Conflicted, I sat in my study and tried to reconcile two warring selves: the lover of literature and women who sees *Cosmo* as superficial and one-dimensional with the writer in me who longs for the larger audience that this magazine's several million readers might bring my work. I tried to remember the last time I'd read *Cosmo*. An image of myself, age nineteen, before a newsstand at the University of California. A cup of cappuccino in one hand, red licorice in the other, I pondered the cornucopia of magazines on my study break from comparative literature class. We were studying the tragic heroine Antigone, from Sophocles through modern writers. At the newsstand I was preoccupied with Antigone's choice to bury her brother's corpse, thus rejecting her uncle, King Creon, and his mandate forbidding any burial of her traitor-brother. Steadfastly, Antigone refused to put a public face on what she knew was false. For performing her brother's burial rites, Antigone was sentenced by Creon to herself be buried alive in a cave.

*What's a girl to do?* I found myself thinking guiltily. Maybe it was the strong caffeine, the knot of licorice in my stomach, but standing there gazing at row after row of women's magazines, each proclaiming a body, a hair color, an outfit, a mood change, a style, all to bring out "the real you," I found myself laughing a little too loudly. There were no moral choices here—only questions of what makeup or blouse, what hem length or hairstyle. It was when I was in this state of mind that my hand reached for a copy of *Cosmopolitan.*

As I flipped through its pages, I barely fended off an allergy attack brought on by the heavy brew of perfume ads. I read an article that was a variation on the theme does-he-love-you: ways-to-make-sure; then I glanced through the beauty hints and fashion displays. I forgot all about Antigone. All I could think of was my boyfriend who, the week before, had made the decision—was it a moral choice?—to sleep with another woman when I said I wouldn't drop out of school and move to Canada with him to avoid the Vietnam draft. Why had I not chosen to stand by my man, as Helen Gurley Brown always advised, even at the cost of my own educational life? Was Antigone simply standing by her man in burying her brother? If I really loved my boyfriend, wouldn't I have changed my clothes, my hair, my life for him?

I imagined a Platonic dialogue between Helen Gurley Brown and Antigone:

HGB:  Do you want to be single and shut off in a cave for the rest of your life? Isn't it enough already that your father slept with his mother, put out his own eyes (what kind of touch-up could ever cover *that?*), and now you have to heap more tragedy down on your pretty head by defying Creon's order? Simply put your royal garb back on and sit beside Creon as the true princess you are meant to be. May I also suggest a make-over?

ANTIGONE:  I choose to mourn my brother properly, even if it means I will not live to happily marry my beloved Haemon, who, as Creon's son, will one day make me queen. I will never be a queen if I cannot also be human. It is the act of burial that first makes us human.

HGB:  If burial is what makes us human, my dear, then why not simply bury your feelings?

That was about as far as I got at the magazine stand all those many years ago before the perfume sampler pages did overwhelm me. *What's a girl to do?* I asked myself again these two decades later on my second close encounter with *Cosmo*. I hadn't thought of Antigone in a long time, and I never thought of Helen Gurley Brown. In fact, I assumed she had also long passed away into myth. The thought of this living legend reading my story and giving her almighty yes or no took on a personal drama I had not expected.

On an impulse, I took out a tarot deck that a friend

had given me, along with *The Tarot Handbook* by anthropologist Angeles Arrien. Although fascinated by tarot, I'd never really explored it much myself. Shuffling inexpertly, I drew a breath and a card. Queen of Cups. It was a good sign, I thought, reading Arrien's commentary:

> The Queen of Cups represents the constant practice of owning one's feelings and expressing them without blame or judgment. She does not abandon, deny, or repress her feelings. She does not use her feelings to attack others nor does she apologize for her feelings ... she chooses integrity over illusion or deception ... Whatever she is feeling inside, she is determined to reflect accurately any dichotomy between what is felt internally and what is being expressed externally.

The Queen of Cups, come to think of it, sounded a lot like Antigone. That afternoon, I bought a copy of *Cosmo* and placed the Queen of Cups on top of it. An interesting juxtaposition, this regal tarot queen of watery reflection atop a *Cosmo* cover girl, pretty in pink. The Queen of Cups gleams in pale sea-blue robes, sunlight circling her hair like a halo crown. In one hand she holds a stork, symbol of all births, from new ideas to new life. With the other arm she embraces a crayfish shell. The watery double reflection that mirrors this Neptunian queen shows that she is in equipoise with her own heart, expressing her feelings clearly—"as above, so below."

If the Queen of Cups was an accurate mirror of a pure stream of feelings above as below, did this mean that queens are like real people? Does a queen have a responsibility to reflect her subjects, to mirror their realities, to

open her heart to all the people? To discuss such feminine questions I, like Antigone turning to her sister,
Ismene, for counsel, turned to my sister Paula.

"The queen!" my sister exulted when she heard that
Helen Gurley Brown was making the final pass on my
story. "She's a woman's woman. She's beautiful *and*
smart. She hasn't had to choose between the two ..."
Paula hesitated. What she did not add, what we both were
pondering at that moment was the fact that in our family
my sister was dubbed the beauty and I, the student. She
was our father's princess, I was my mother's hope. Having a father for mentor meant that my sister had chosen
nursing over medical school and given up her secret
longing to become an actress. *It is one of the saddest things*
*of my life,* my sister once told me. *That I made my choices to*
*please Father, instead of myself.* And I had chosen to be a
writer, well aware that my mother gave up her writing
when she gave birth to me.

"Like we chose," I finished for my sister.

"Like we *used* to choose," my sister corrected. "Before
we finally got away from home."

I remembered exactly the day we first discovered it,
my sister and I. She was visiting me in my college dorm,
down from her own freshman year upstate. She sat on my
bunk bed and eyed me critically. At last she pronounced
with the dignity of a decree of freedom: "I know something incredible now! I'm smart too. And you're also
pretty."

It seemed the greatest sacrilege at the time. I even
fought her off, but she would have none of it. "We are
*both*," she said triumphantly. But still she whispered.

We each glanced around to make sure no one had

heard our little conceit, lest we be thought victim of the dread disease "a swollen head," which my father always direly warned us against.

My close call with getting a swollen head over the dizzying idea that *Cosmo* would indeed publish my story was quickly over. After her weekend read of my novel, Brown told her editors she was concerned about the ending. It was not happy; it was, in fact, "downbeat."

Rejected, I found myself again standing in front of the magazine rack at my local Safeway. There they all were, those smart, beautiful women carelessly eyeing me from every cover: the casually elegant *Vogue* woman off to a Riviera weekend with her favorite designer; the stunningly studied, natural ingenues of *Mademoiselle;* the sassy smarties of *New Woman* and *Working Woman;* the sophisticates of *Elle* and *Vanity Fair.* With the notable exception of *Ms.,* I felt utterly alien.

Perhaps I was scowling or, worse, downbeat. Whatever my expression, it was enough to elicit a breezy command from a man who reached for *Popular Mechanics* and said, "Smile!"

I looked him straight in the eye. "I've just come from a funeral."

Then, and only then, did I smile. With casual elegance I turned away from the women's magazines and plunged into the real world of *Time.* The first page I turned to was a little blurb in the "Milestones: Recovering" section. Yet another movie star had checked herself into the Betty Ford Center for drug and alcohol treatment.

I shivered: Betty Ford was one of our country's ex-queens. Unlike Antigone, Betty Ford had smiled when she wanted to weep. All during her husband's reign, she chose the public face over the cave, with all its interior shadows. Only after leaving office, with its Happy Face and often uninspired honorary duties of a First Lady, had Betty Ford admitted her addictions. Now her rehabilitation center is shared with others who have suffered the same loss of Self—those public people who arrive looking like blackened, used-up firecracker shells, refuse of their own dazzling performances. I wondered, standing there with those women's magazine faces all smiling out at me, What do the women look like in the Betty Ford Center? What happens in that labyrinth of private soul-searching after a lifetime of smiling performance? In that underworld Betty Ford has opened to others, is there solace at last in feeling? Is another first sign of our being human the choice to go into the cave—a symbolic death and burial—to arise again, redeemed not by the false transcendence of an "upbeat" feminine face but by the deepening calm and claim of one's own inner life and darkness?

There is nothing upbeat about exploring one's own darkness. The feminine descent is not yet seen as a valid counterpoint to the hero's journey to Hell and back. But if we as women are to stand by ourselves and our men, doesn't that imply an equal journey into the underworld? Why then must we, like our First Ladies, literally lift our faces in the relentlessly cheerful public smile?

First Ladies, queens, and women's magazines are all feminine models—as above, so below. What have the recent decades of First Ladies modeled for us? When we look to find ourselves, our choices, our responsibilities mirrored in them, do they authentically return to us that

Queen of Cups equipoise? Do they offer us a feminine role that has the moral dignity, the depth of a woman who reflects accurately the inner feelings with the world of appearance?

The last decades of First Ladies offer us instead a litany of sadness postponed, of bodies dismembered, of psyches drugged into smiling sublimation: Betty Ford's cheerful commute between tranquilizers and liquor; zippy Kitty Dukakis drinking a nearly suicidal dose of rubbing alcohol in a postelection bout with her cross-addictions. Then there is the fact that Pat Nixon, Betty Ford, and Nancy Reagan all had mastectomies while in office. Nancy Reagan's much-debated anorexia, Barbara Bush's overactive thyroid condition with its symptomatic nervousness and mood swings suggest that the upbeat presidential style has a downside when it comes to the feminine body.

What does it mean metaphorically that the risk of breast cancer (already an alarming one out of four) is more than twice as high (three of the most recent five) if one is a First Lady? In the book *Tree*, Deena Metzger traces her own healing from breast cancer surgery. "I will tell you a secret," she writes. "I have always believed that quiet kills, that cancer comes from silence." What might have happened if those First Ladies who lost a breast had not been silenced by their roles? Did we ever publicly hear those women's lament over losing those breasts, symbols of nurturance? Is mourning somehow nurturing to our feminine souls? Can public mourning, such as Antigone's ritual grief in defiance of the ruling male command to be silent, also teach us lessons we need to survive?

My sister, a surgical nurse, says that if you want to find an exclusive club for women, go to any hospital waiting room. "Men wait for babies," she remarks. "Women wait for all the rest. We do it rather well. There's an art to receiving bad news, to grieving, and accepting loss." One thinks of a Greek chorus as so many women in a waiting room. When they mourn, we see wisdom, holy outrage, humility, surrender, and compassion—all gifts of grief. As women, if we do not allow ourselves these gifts, we condemn ourselves to being imitation men. In my imagination, I will always see Pat Nixon, Betty Ford, and Nancy Reagan in a one-breasted Amazonian stance beside their husbands. And I see Betty Ford and Kitty Dukakis stumbling, falling from grace in a long, drugged, slow-motion descent. Then there is Barbara Bush, the day before her husband declared an air war on Iraq. Very much on the ground, Mrs. Bush lost control of her sled and broke her leg. "She doesn't know why she didn't bail out," her press secretary told *The New York Times*. "She just held on, and, the next thing she knew, there was the tree." The article notes that the First Lady was "smiling through the pain." As a metaphor for self-destruction, her descent and physical injury, hours before her husband launched our country headlong into a devastating war, shows the cost of a woman carrying both her own and her husband's shadow with a smile.

The cost can eventually claim a woman's life. After Kitty Dukakis's attempted suicide, *Time* quoted an editor friend of the Dukakis family as saying, "Kitty had to do the mourning for both of them." He was referring to Michael Dukakis's humiliating presidential election defeat. But the pattern is not simply one of loss. It is an accumulation of First Ladies cheerfully carrying their husbands' shadows. The feminine body shows the stress. A *Boston Globe* reporter commented on the Dukakises' not untypical roles: "The governor is so stoic. The burden was more on Kitty. Someone said, 'When you hit Michael, Kitty bleeds.' Basically, right now Kitty is hemorrhaging."

Is it a woman's job to bleed to death while standing smilingly by her man? Or to catapult into a tree? Or to lose a breast, a symbolic half of what nurtures our bodies, our creations? Are women on a collision course if we cannot claim our normal sadness, if we cannot, like Antigone, make public the sorrow that the king forbids himself, his women, and finally his nation? When King Creon forbade his nephew decent burial, the country was divided against him. What Creon didn't allow, what our country's leaders still can't embrace is that grief can bring a country together. It can teach us that we are one, not only in war or triumph but also in sharing our sorrow.

One First Lady who fully claimed and so helped us carry a nation's grief was Jacqueline Kennedy. She could not avoid the grief, as if it were a bullet that missed her. We all witnessed her as she crawled over the limousine, blood-splattered in pink, screaming. We all watched her at her husband's funeral as she held a child's hand in each of hers, face wide open to mourning. Unexpectedly, I caught sight of her very near that funeral day. We lived in Virginia, and my parents, although they had not voted for Kennedy, took us to the procession.

On a ceremonial black horse, our fallen leader's gleaming brown boots rode backward in the stirrups. Following was a black limousine, moving with slow dignity. It seemed an eternity as I, a twelve-year-old, stood there on the curb. Most of the adults missed it, my direct view into the limo in which Jacqueline Kennedy rode between John-John and Caroline. I noticed that John-John was fractious, jumping around the expanse of car. Caroline sat with her hands folded in her lap, head down. Jacqueline stared straight ahead, her black veil shadowing but not hiding the tears that simply streamed endlessly down her face. I have never seen such undisguised grief. Its clarity took my breath away, as if I'd fallen from a great height to the ground. For a long time after I saw that grave face, I was silent. Later, when I told my siblings what I'd seen, I surprised myself by saying under my breath, "She was ... she was ... beautiful."

Beautiful not like after a face-lift, not like with a forced and false smile. Beautiful not like a drugged, upbeat actor's wife with one breast sacrificed to the cause. But beautiful like an open heart, full and flowing.

"If in our culture men can't cry," a friend of mine remarked, "there is also this: Men are never required to show joy when they don't feel it."

Another friend, a psychotherapist added, "Many women in session will smile at the exact point when they are in the most pain. They are frightened they will be punished if they show their true feelings. That punishment may be emotional abandonment or rejection or anger at the woman's refusal to cover up the truth, *her* truth."

Antigone again. And who helps the ruler Creon in this modern play but *Cosmo* and all the other women's magazines that steadily churn out issue after issue of that one dictum that so belittles and dismembers us: *Smile.*

"You have no idea how many women come into my office and simply cry—for hours, for weeks, for years." This, from another psychotherapist friend. "Sometimes I go through a box of Kleenex every day. And I wonder—do women cry so much because men can't, or is this just a feminine and perfectly appropriate response to the world?"

In her popular book *Copper Woman*, Anne Cameron retells the stories of a secret society of Native women on Vancouver Island, BC. In one story, Copper Woman, lonely after her godly teachers have left her, began to weep so inconsolably that her abundant tears and mucus made a "mess" in the sand. She tried to kick over it, bury it. Then the magic women told her "not to feel shame, not to bury the snot, but to save it, even cherish it, and when she had learned to accept even this most gross evidence of her own mortality, then from the acceptance would come the means whereby she would never again be alone, never again be lonely." Sure enough, the mucus mess came alive as Snot Boy, who grew to become her lover. Their union created a daughter. When at last Copper Woman beheld her daughter, she "felt the loneliness diminish until it was no larger than a small round pebble on the beach."

If instead of simplistic women's magazines, our country still had women's secret societies like those Native councils—many of whom had to approve any war their men might make—would we have inherited the image of our elders, our public First Ladies expressing a full spectrum of emotions, from sorrow to joy? Would we believe in a Great Mother who cried all of us humans into being?

"Women have a genius for feeling," my sister once told me. "I see it every day in those waiting rooms. I push open the surgery doors and pray that I will be able to tell the news to a woman."

Antigone, when speaking of Creon's injunction, tells her sister, Ismene, "It's not for him to keep me from my own." Ismene, who does not follow her sister's lead in burying their brother, laments, "So I shall ask of them beneath the earth forgiveness, for in these things I am forced, and shall obey the men in power." Sadly, Antigone answers her sister's decision, "I know I please those whom I most should please."

Antigone is talking about the gods who, in Greek times, were male and female, showed every emotion, from the basest envy to the most sublime mercies. It is ironic that in an ancient civilization that refused women full social status, the Greeks' myths still reflected feminine rights and powers. Our current one-dimensional father-godhead excludes the wide emotional range and many faces of the Greek myths, which granted the feminine its divinity. Because this Christian father-god model mirrors only half of our humanity, we are less whole. Without the model of a god-mother, how do women find their divinity? How do we learn to value our feminine birthrights, our emotional gifts? Did God the Father grieve the sacrifice of his only Son? There's not much about it in our scriptures. That chore was left to his mother at the foot of the cross and to Mary Magdalene, who wept right up until she saw that the stone in front of the tomb was rolled away. One line in the Bible is the simplest to memorize: "Jesus wept." He was a "man of sorrows." How did that masculine grief get translated into a world of people smiling through their pain and marching to one rather military beat—the upbeat?

The definition of the word *upbeat* is "an unaccented beat, especially immediately preceding a downbeat." Is there any music without the up and the down movement? If we are to walk with only one foot, what will be the crutch that must take the place of that balancing foot—alcohol, drugs, the denial of death? In a recent Ann Landers column, a World War II veteran writes that he is concerned about the health of Martha Raye, whom he has just seen on TV at an awards ceremony. She is in a wheelchair. The vet recalls Raye's performance for his Second Armored Division during the war's North African campaign. Before her show, Raye tripped on a "hastily constructed outdoor stage. She suffered a painful ankle injury but refused to have a doctor check it out until after she had put on a terrific show for the 20,000 assembled soldiers." Although the veteran doesn't express it, I wonder whether his concern for Miss Raye is mixed with some shame, some guilt that the woman who sang and smiled and danced on an injured ankle might never heal. Has the old wound finally caught up and crippled her so that she cannot walk now at all? Ann Landers answers by sending a call out: "Martha, let's hear from you. We want to know that you are OK." Will Ann Landers print her answer if it is not upbeat?

Martha Raye and Barbara Bush in wheelchairs, Kitty Dukakis grinning as she leaves the hospital—all our First Ladies smiling through the pain. In a 1988 poll on the First Lady by *Ladies' Home Journal,* readers responded to this question: "Do you think that a First Lady should ever publicly disagree with the president on controversial issues?" Sixty-nine percent said, "The president's wife should keep her opinions to herself." This majority is not ruling men silencing women, it is women passing the message on to their daughters: Continue to deny your own truth if it differs from public (masculine) policy.

Does a First Lady of moral principles such as Antigone or a master of emotional integrity such as the Queen of Cups have any welcome among women in our country? There are signs of change. Though all of our First Ladies have relinquished any career to stand by their presidential men, some of them returned to fulfilling jobs after serving their terms. Jacqueline Kennedy Onassis in her role as Doubleday editor recently published *The Power of Myth* based on the popular PBS series of Bill Moyers interviews with Joseph Campbell.

Recently Washington columnist Marianne Means raised the question of a First Lady continuing her profession during her White House years. Though Barbara Bush has never held a paying job, her second lady (in waiting), Marilyn Quayle, is "reportedly restless, feeling underutilized and missing the satisfaction of using her mental skills in a profession [law] for which she was trained." Marilyn Quayle and her sister are now at work on a novel. Such precedents may soon lead to a revised role for First Ladies that reflects more accurately the realities of the millions of working women today.

In the First Ladies of the nineties we may witness a trend similar to that just now affecting the women's magazines. *The New York Times* reported in May 1991 that a few farsighted magazines, such as *Mirabella, Countryside, Harper's Bazaar,* and *New Choices,* were hiring "regular people" rather than "bone-thin models." "We like faces that look like road maps," says a *Countryside* editor. "We felt from the beginning that part of our editorial thrust was to find real faces." These real faces might not always smile, they might show real feelings. Perhaps we can expect in the near future an article by a First Lady that quotes Dostoevsky's hero in *The Possessed,* who says simply that what you must do to establish emotional balance and integrity in our world is to "bear your own burden."

One of the most important models ever given me as a woman ironically enough came from my own father. Although he never liked it when faced with the example in his daughters, he did teach us, "Be like water. Water is gentle enough to follow every curve in the Earth. But when it rises up, nothing is more powerful."

What we need now is a mythology as natural and elemental as water: one that shows us women who are crowned queens not for obeying masculine orders to deny their feelings, their divinity, their inner knowing, their shadowy caves but for claiming their genius at feelings, at experiencing the dark knowledge of our own and others' natures. If God the Mother, like Copper Woman, cried all into creation, then are those millions of women weeping in therapy sessions all over the world embodying the divine? Is the acceptance of our smallness, our humanness what in the end makes us divine? Is true heroism the ability to cry over a fallen brother, a broken leg, a lost breast, a country?

In the end, King Creon was yielding as water. But he cried alone. Antigone hung herself in the cave to which he condemned her; his son Haemon fell on his own sword and died embracing Antigone's body. Creon's wife, upon hearing of her son's suicide, took her own knife out and ended her queenly reign. Grief struck Creon at last, and too late. He was left with no one to share his feelings. "My life is warped past cure," he mourned and disappeared. The chorus concluded, "Our happiness depends on wisdom all the way."

True wisdom, as the Greeks also told us, is knowing oneself. Between the knowing and the public speaking of our truths lies the vast, uncharted territory of the emotions. The clear and reflective watery realm of the Queen of Cups might be a guide if we are to avoid repeating tragedies. The feminine skills of emotional authenticity, if claimed, can help us all, men and women, to find that full humanity that is grounded not in false transcendence but in sobering self-knowledge.

I like to think that sometime in the future a woman who is a modern Antigone might be a cover girl. At the very least, I make a plea for a First Lady like Eleanor Roosevelt to pass our way again. Her husband was in a wheelchair and Eleanor wasn't always smiling. Maybe it will take another Depression to make us admit the downbeat. Maybe it will take a national loss like Kennedy's or Creon's. Whatever it will take, I suspect the end of the Stoics will come upon us with slow certainty. May we meet that time with the dignity of a Greek chorus, a waiting room full of women long practiced in the healing and creative art of life-giving tears.

# GIFT OF THE MAGI
# CUPCAKES

In the South of my childhood, food and fellowship was love. At Christmas there had to be an abundance or else we thought ourselves pitiful. I don't remember Christmas presents so much as I do the food and presence of certain people who have come to embody this holiday for me.

In those early days, grandparents abounded, not only grandparents but great-grandparents, two of whom I knew until I was almost ten. My great-grandmother Thomas was a fierce but dreamy presence. Her wedding ring, which I inherited, was made for her by Great-grandfather; it is a dark cameo of Diana, the goddess of the hunt, childbirth, and the moon. Great-grandmother Thomas encompassed all three: She shot the wild Christmas turkeys or ducks, she bore four quite bold sons and a pensive daughter, and she had a way of looking at the world with a visionary clarity as if she saw people and their inner landscapes revealed, but by moonlight.

One of the things Great-grandmother saw quite clearly was that at Christmas there must be much celebration of miracles and mysteries. That's why, to this day, her recipe for Christmas chowchow has never been revealed, even by my grandmother, who still makes this tongue-tingling relish do to turkey what salsa does to pale tortillas. Perhaps it was Great-grandmother Thomas who started our family tradition of making our own moccasins on Christmas Eve, out of whatever the men had shot and tanned during the year. To sneak around the house way past midnight on Christmas Eve in mooseskin moccasins with our own bright beadwork was, to us children, a way of meeting the grown-ups' penchant for mystery with a bit of our own.

My grandmother Elsie has continued her mother's Christmas traditions by making a divinity that arouses more religious feeling than do many Christmas pageants. Grandmother is mysterious about this recipe, too. It is a sugary-stiff, white-hard fudge, studded with Georgia black walnuts—those strangely bitter, smoky nuts that seemed somehow like illegal aliens to us children, perhaps because of all the fuss about bringing them up from Georgia, as if smuggled over the border by odd Mrs. Phoebe, the only supplier of Georgia black walnuts we knew. The arrangements to pick up the nuts were clandestine: middle-of-the-night drop-off points and the burlap bag of black walnuts hidden more diligently than any of our Christmas presents. To open those hard-shelled nuts was a minor miracle itself: Father placed them under a plywood board and then ran over them repeatedly with the beat-up Buick station wagon.

That was Grandmother's divinity, the petite madeleine of my childhood Christmas. But it was not the only holiday sweet. Mother added her cherry and pineapple fudge, her peanut-butter fruitcake, homemade nougat, and caramel popcorn balls, all served with eggnog or Russian tea. A heathen once brought bourbon balls to our home, and we had gobbled half a dozen apiece before Mother could swoop down on them and deliver them over to the fate of all liquor in our house—down the drain. As the bourbon balls gurgled in the newfangled garbage disposal, we children spun around the tree, tipsy and stringing cranberries.

So that later the same evening when we were bundled up to go out into the crystal cold of that Christmas Eve to witness a live nativity scene, it did not surprise us a bit. In fact it seemed quite in keeping with the spirits of that evening and the bourbon balls that as the teenage Mary appeared astride her lowly donkey and shyly approached the little lean-to barn where awaited a shivering gaggle of angels, wise men, and shepherds—she struck awe in us. We were moved by this modern Mary who calmed herself by blowing incandescent pink veils with each breath and her bubble gum.

After that Christmas epiphany, bubble gum became a staple of our stockings, a little ritual that my Catholic friends, who usually cornered the market on Mother Mary, miracles, and other saints, had to envy. It had never occurred to us before seeing that live nativity, that Mary, the mother of such an important baby, might have been frightened or felt alone of all her kind at Christmas. In fact, anybody being frightened or alone at Christmas seemed incongruous to us—though the adults were always hauling us off to progressive holiday dinners with the "shut-ins," as we heard them described.

Progressive dinners proceed from house to house, potluck course to course, and at Christmas there was often caroling in between, say, the orgy of hors d'oeuvres and the Caesar salad. Not just the usual carols; we sang spriggets of that year's Christmas cantata.

One year we even got so bold as to take our taste treats and Christmas cantata to the great St. Elizabeth's mental institution up in Washington, DC. The cantata was called "Night of Miracles," and the treats were called Gift of the Magi Cupcakes: chocolate on chocolate on chocolate, kind of like the original sin of chocolates. Some of us sang that cantata with dark-stained lips from sampling what should have gone to the shut-ins.

The inmates gathered in a circle, all dolled up for our visit. They nodded and tapped feet like normal folk, and we decided they weren't mad at all. I suppose we expected to see people transformed into pigs like in the Bible or someone foaming at the mouth. But they all ate their cupcakes and clapped, just like a go-to-church audience. All, that is, except a very small and very old lady with two bright splotches of rouge that endeared her to me because of Mary of the Pink Veils. She, alone of all women, peeled her Gift of the Magi Cupcakes with delicate, white lace gloves and then, smiling pretty as you please, as we belted out the rousing chorus of "Night of Miracles," this little lady smashed her cupcake atop her head.

I was so startled I forgot to sing, and all the way home

I pondered this mystery. Was she adorning herself with food the way children do or the way we'd seen old people in nursing homes practically wear our imported Christmas peaches? I'd seen old people peck and nod happily over those peaches that didn't require putting in teeth. Was that little lace lady happy, too? Or was that cupcake anointment her own personal miracle? When I asked my grandmother, she said what Great-grandmother Thomas might have said: that everyone has his or her own way of celebrating Christmas and all we had to do was be there to see it, like the shepherds, the angels, and those other assembled witnesses who watched by moonlight. Then Grandmother went back to stuffing the wild duck that, the next time I saw it, would be glazed on a Christmas platter, its innards filled with apples and onions.

Parsnips in brown sugar, crocks of homemade hominy, sweet potatoes, red cabbage slaw, some kind of guessing-game salad we call heavenly hash—it will all be there again this Christmas. My grandmother, at ninety, still cooks her mother's Christmas chowchow, and her divinity is already in the mail.

If Grandmother were here in my kitchen this Christmas, she would ask me whom I've fed or sung to, and what personal miracles I've witnessed. She would not ask me if I am happy; happiness is another one of those things meant to be a mystery. Grandmother would ask only that on Christmas no one be hungry, or alone of all their kind—and no celebration be unseen.

# POWER IN THE BLOOD

O n a blithe spring afternoon in the late 1970s, I sat with my little sister in an East Coast women's clinic gazing at an obscure black-and-white photo of her unborn child. In the ultrasound, her baby was the size of a tadpole.

"Do you know," my sister said, her eyes brimming, "that the fetus goes through *every* step of an evolutionary process ... from fish to reptile—with a tail and everything—to mammal? It's amazing."

"Yes," I said softly, sadly, "amazing."

We didn't say another word; we'd gone round and round for days. Father deserted, mother barely making it, how would she support this new life?

At last my sister said simply, "I just can't do it ... *not* again."

Again would have been her second abortion. "But," my sister continued soberly, "what will happen to this baby if I don't?"

I opened my mouth to begin the bargaining, the advising, the begging—can you bring this child into a life unsupported, unwanted? But instead I fell absolutely still as nausea swept over me—the way I'd felt when I found myself pregnant seven years before, a baby my body mercifully miscarried. The way I'd felt the summer after my own spontaneous abortion, when I came home from college to find my mother sitting too still in our living room.

It was also a sunny, seemingly benign afternoon as my mother sat motionless, listening the way blind people do to better navigate their world by some inner sonar.

"I'm forty-one years old," my mother had said quietly, "raised all four of you kids. I can't start making babies all over again."

It was 1970, *Roe* v. *Wade* was three years away. All we knew was that my mother was again pregnant, that her Southern Baptist religion and our state rigorously forbade abortion, that another child was not only unwise in a family of four teenagers but unhealthy for my mother, both physically and psychologically.

"I never wanted this many," my mother breathed, as if talking to herself, as if I were not there, the first of her unwanted.

"I know" was what I said, wavering between old rage and newfound understanding. Only six months before I'd found myself in her condition. And the irony of finding myself pregnant at twenty—the exact age my mother got pregnant with me—didn't escape me. Here we sat together, mother and firstborn, twenty years after my conception, debating the fate of another child.

Time was turning back upon itself, as if we two had

become all women in some secret society, talking quietly about birth and death—matters that belonged to us, body and soul. But now there were the laws, the sins, the crimes that we must consider.

"Do you," Mother began, trembling, "you *must* know someone ... one of those radical friends who's against the Vietnam War or something."

"I don't know how to get an abortion, Mother, if that's what you're asking. But ... but I can ask around."

Suddenly Mother laughed, a hoarse sound more like a cry. "Nowadays mothers have to ask daughters about these things. Used to be a time ... my own grandmother told me once, when there were herbs a woman could use ... potions. Used to be a woman knew because her mother taught her secretly." Then she laughed again, and it was a scary sound, like coughing. It reminded me that, even though I was grown now, all my childhood Mother had frightened me with her dark moods. She'd also fascinated me, because alternating with her furies was an exuberance so bright it eclipsed most of my friends' mothers. She was charming and she was dangerous; she was brilliant and feline and trapped. The atmosphere around her was always charged, charismatic, electric, but somehow short-circuited. All of her children wondered what she might have been without us, this mother who before marriage, during the war, ran off to work a man's job and who still had dreams of a career. A decade later she would live this dream. But my mother's future fulfillment was still unborn that summer afternoon as we sat rocking opposite each other in our La-Z-Boys.

"I did try some of those old wives' ways," Mother told me, and her face paled. "But I couldn't remember how ..."

My hands shook as if I already knew what she would say. "I tried them on you. Of course, I didn't know it was *you* inside, and now that I know you I'm glad it didn't work …"

I caught my breath and managed to say, "I might have done that, too, Mother." But my heart was racing.

"Well, didn't work isn't exactly right …" She wasn't looking at me.

And then she told the story: how she tried everything until at last, in desperation—because she'd gotten pregnant on her honeymoon, because they were too young, too poor—she inflicted upon herself an abortion. All night she crouched in a bathtub full of lukewarm, bloody water. How she sobbed; how solitary was her suffering. And the horror when she discovered soon after that she was still pregnant.

I did not weep that sunny day as my mother did. I felt physical shock, repulsion, and a familiar longing. Everything made terrible sense.

"Can you ever forgive me?" my mother asked and held her soft, rounding belly.

"That's not up to me," I heard myself answer, as if from a great distance.

Two weeks later she called me at school to report in a subdued voice that she had been wrong. She was not pregnant, after all. And, again, would I forgive her?

"I won't forgive myself," my little sister was saying, calling me back to her, as we sat in the women's clinic. "I don't think I could, not again."

My sister did not have that abortion. The child I first saw as a tadpole is now almost twelve; he has two other siblings. And my sister spends every free moment—when she is not home schooling her children because she objects to public education—sitting in picket lines wearing her white nurse's uniform and demonstrating against abortions.

What happened? What drove my sister to sit on picket lines and in jail? I think of her in a prison cell heckled by inmates for still clutching her JESUS LOVES THE LITTLE CHILDREN sign; then I see her bailed out by sister soldiers, only to herself heckle women crossing their pro-life protest lines. Why this war of the women? What made my sister turn on herself and decide her own earlier abortion was immoral?

It began right after her second child. After years of supporting herself and her first son, my sister married his legitimate father, and a year later they had another son. At this point she cut back her nursing work schedule to part-time, devoting herself to mothering. It was during this mothering that she followed the family trend of southern fundamentalism to its more extreme faction: home schooling and fervent pro-life activism. By the time she bore her third child, she was carrying him on her hip and arguing earnestly with tearful teenagers as they hesitated outside doors of women's clinics.

When my sister was jailed for the first time, I wondered, Who were those fundamentalist friends who had so influenced her? Were they all housewives and mothers stripped of the prestige they once had as professional women? Because the world so little honored them as mothers, did they have to elevate motherhood to a sacrament and the choice against it to a sacrilege? Were these pro-life women so dependent on men—husbands' salaries or unsteady child support—that they felt the furious righteousness of any minority? Were they waging war because they believed their lives and way of life endangered?

What I felt most from my sister, beneath her zeal and anger, was fear. Of whom? Of what? And then one day, when she and I were talking about our inherited family fear of flying, I understood only too well. Our brother, whom we believe immune from our phobia because he hurls himself straight into it with his career as a navy aviator, was gently lecturing his three older sisters. He concluded simply, "When you get on a plane, just put yourself in God's hands."

We responded to our brother's logic with resigned silence. How could he know? The men in our family practically live on planes; the women stay below, bearing children, writing stories, and watching the sky with fear and trembling. Why? Is it something deeper than just a family phobia? Could it be that our feminine fear of the sky is an ancient terror? What came from the sky to frighten us, to make us as women so wary of leaving the Earth?

"How many women pilots in the navy, little brother?" my middle sister asked. When my brother balked, she said, "I guess we'll all be in that sky of yours soon enough."

And then I felt it: the fear. It's a smell, something hidden that sets free its scent, sweet and festering. Then I understood that my youngest sister's fear as she sits on those abortion lines is a public mirror of the fear we three sisters share from our fundamentalist childhood. For when my sister faces those young women contemplating the doors of the abortion clinic, she doesn't really see them at all. Who my sister faces is her God. And He finds her sorely lacking.

This God lives in the sky, not on the Earth. He is God the Father, without God the Mother. He has an only son; He has no daughters. And it is this masculine God we were all as children taught to fear. So why not also fear the sky where this God dwells—where our brother and father, but not mother or sisters, are welcome?

Though we were not arguing abortion that day, it was the first time I realized how profoundly this fundamentalist fear haunts the pro-life women. And it told me that, at core, abortion is a spiritual issue with two sides who are not speaking the same language. How can a woman carrying the sign JESUS HEARS THEIR TINY SCREAMS converse with another whose sign states ABORTION—EVERY WOMAN'S BIRTHRIGHT? It's like a screaming match between two tribes who offend each other simply because they occupy the same territory—in this case, a woman's body. To the pro-choice advocates, their fundamentalist sisters might as well be speaking in tongues; and to the pro-life true believers, their sisters are denying them dialogue on the only real issue—and that's not women, it's God.

Since my sister is family, I search for some common language. But I cannot speak freedom when she speaks salvation; I cannot talk personal conscience when she answers with Bible verses. It hurts me when my pro-choice friends dismiss my sister as a fanatic; and it troubles me when my sister declares that my friends who've had abortions are murderers.

Is there any place we meet? Is there any translation so that both sides can at least stop and understand each other, even identify some common ground? My personal journey to understand my sister and myself takes me first to family history and then to feminine history itself.

"Do you think she really believes she's going straight to Hell because she had an abortion ten years ago?" I ask my middle sister after our sister's latest pro-life march on Washington, DC.

"Yes," this sister says flatly. "Of course. I mean, her religion has her on trial for murder. And guess what? She lost her case a long time ago."

"Found guilty," I say and feel again the fear. I used to think I could leave it in childhood, but I know now it will always be with me at some level, just as I will always feel uneasy when I step onto an airplane. I often remember: we three stair-step sisters, legs dangling in a pew, our shoulders hunched over as if awaiting a blow. The preacher shouts: *It was you who killed Him, sister, and me, brother, and every man, woman, child born. We killed Him. We surely did. We hung Him up on that cross where we all shoulda been.*

"Yes," my sister murmurs as I tell her this memory. "We're just born murderers."

Then I remember: pro-life marchers with their plastic baby dolls strung up on coat hangers, those small bodies splashed with painted blood. Tiny crucifixions. How did the fetus come to replace Christ on the cross?

"I'm sick of blood and crosses," I blurt to my sister, feeling slightly blasphemous. "Women are bleeding, too. I did, you did."

This sister, also a nurse and mother of three, found out during her fourth pregnancy that she carried a dead fetus. During the abortion, the gynecologist punctured her uterus, then rushed her to the hospital, where he proceeded to puncture her bladder. She survived to become pregnant a fifth time, though any pregnancy for her is now life-threatening. This summer she suffered a miscarriage. She bled for a week, quietly going about her days as if this were not the death of a child, the end of her childbearing. "It's so hard," she'd said. "I love bringing babies into the world. I'm *good* at it."

Now on the phone she says softly, "Yes, there is a lot of women's blood in our family."

"Power in the blood!" I aim for black humor but instead feel sad as I quote the Baptist hymn that summons again our childhood:

> Would you be free of your burden of sin?
> There's power, power, wonder-working power
> In the precious blood of the Lamb.

The Lamb in this hymn is not a fetus, it is Christ bleeding on the cross. Anyone who understands fundamentalism in this country knows that this is a religion steeped in the Old Testament God. Christ is sacrifice and savior, but rarely can those paradoxical New Testament parables compete with the worldly, familiar fury of Jehovah. Christ, by comparison, seems downright feminine, unworldly. Had Christ been a divine daughter, forswearing the sword, tribal, virginal, sowing neither seeds nor war but words, the enigma of such a presence might have been better understood, during that time as well as now. But the feminine in Jehovah's Son is unrecognized, just as the feminine counterpart of Jehovah is missing.

Is it any coincidence, then, that this more feminine

New Testament Christ is also missing from those pro-life crosses? When did bloody fetuses usurp Christ's sacrifice? Do fetuses fulfill His role—to bring redemption and forgiveness? Do the pro-life women carry their own crosses because their role as mother is the only salvation God the Father allows them? And just who are they really trying to save? Themselves? If these women made themselves in Jehovah's image, wouldn't they be the *first* to understand sacrificing a child because sacrificial death in the New Testament brings eternal life?

To understand myself and my sister, I've begun searching for answers to all these questions on the abortion issue, which so haunts my family. I wondered: When did all this power and blood and rebirth come together in our religion? Recently, there has appeared a well-documented body of scholarship on the ancient cultures whose spiritual life was centered in rites of biological motherhood and the Earth as feminine Goddess—Gaia, as the Greeks named her. Today, this Gaia-centered principle is reemerging in fields such as ecology—the Gaia theory that our Earth is a living, self-regulating organism—and religious rites that integrate this primordial feminine deity.

Important research such as Marija Gimbutas's archaeological excavations and study of what she calls "Goddess cultures" in prehistoric European civilizations explores the phenomenon of peaceful Upper Paleolithic and Neolithic cultures (6500–3500 B.C.). The heirs of these Great Mother civilizations are found in the Aegean, Mediterranean, and particularly the Minoan culture of Crete in the second millennium B.C. Gimbutas discovered, "There are no depictions of arms (weapons used against other humans) in any Paleolithic cave paintings. Archaeological evidence of hordes of brutal cavemen just does not exist. There are no remains of weapons used by man against man, no signs of groups of humans being slaughtered." Richard Leakey's research also defines early humans of several million years ago as peaceful and cooperative. These cultures are noted for their flexibility, their egalitarianism, the strong bonds between mothers and children. This was our way of life until about 3000 B.C., with the advent of the Bronze Age and the warrior tribes, with their weapons and their dominating Sky God.

If blood and power didn't first come together in warfare, when were they originally synonymous? In women's blood—and not just the blood of birth. Power was in women's blood from the beginning. The first way we told time was by women's cycles: twenty-eight days between menstruations, twenty-eight days of the Moon's cycle. It was with reverence that our early ancestors greeted their own moon time; it was also with holy ceremony. The Moon was said herself to be "menstruating" as she fulfilled her fertile course, from waxing fullness to waning death to rebirth. Time was not then linear, unrelated, masculine—the minute-to-minute we have today so perfectly symbolized by the digital watch. Everything was in relationship to the circle, the whole. And in the center of this cycle were the Great Mother deities in sync with the Earth's seasons.

Blood rites were originally powerful transformation mysteries. Menstrual blood was sacred, symbolic of the woman's and the Earth's reproductive power. That power, like nature herself, was experienced as both life giving *and* death giving. In those days it was not the God of Genesis but the Great Mother who "giveth and taketh away" and whose name was nevertheless blessed. The root meaning of the word *ritu* or *ritual* is "menstruation." For our ancestors, crossing the threshold from girlhood to womanhood was dramatic and awe inspiring. The wonder of it all: a body bleeds, cleanses, and is reborn. A body does not bleed for nine full moons and so gives birth to another body. How powerful and mysterious, then, this women's blood. Accumulated, it was the essence of creating new life. No wonder this blood was saved, used to fertilize crops, and precious drops offered in only the most important ceremonies.

The Old Testament lamb that was later ritually sacrificed was in imitation of these menstrual rites. Jehovah borrowed power from the feminine blood to make His own ceremonies, just as the male initiation rite of infant or adolescent circumcision cuts a boy's penis to imitate menstruation. How the blessing and power of those early Great Mother cultures' blood became the feminine "curse" and the masculine warfare (blood-shedding) myths of the Old Testament is important. But what is more important is that today we scrutinize the myths we live by to understand our own actions.

The word *hysteria* has its root in the word *womb;* the word *testament* in the word *testicle,* or "male witness." *Hysteria* is now used by psychology to describe feminine dysfunction; *testament* is considered a sacred covenant "between God and man." Thus, the testicles can tell the truth; the womb lies. The truth of the Old Testament is that God, without female mate, created man, who then gave birth to woman from his own body. This is biologically backward from all we know or experience—yet, it is truth, testament. And in a masculine culture, of course, it will be law.

If a woman's womb lies and she is hysterical, isn't it then assumed that she can no more judge who lives and who dies? Is it surprising that she shuts herself off from the company of other equally hysterical women and spends her moon time alone, hiding the signs of her cyclical blood, which is no longer powerful and numinous but cursed?

This summer I spent my first night in a moon lodge. In the Native American tradition, these menstrual huts, the forerunners of masculine sweat lodges, were shelters for feminine cleansing and meditation. A woman's moon time was considered a heightened period of spiritual insight, which the women brought back to benefit the tribe. The women were not outcast; they were in communion. They were not unclean; they were sanctified. Our moon lodge was made by midwives, of bowed willow, red cloth, and earth. It looked like a womb, which we entered crawling on our hands and knees. Inside, lit by candles, the moon lodge was a luminous embrace of silken, scarlet membrane. It was small but spacious. We five women sat cross-legged and murmured, sang, or fell silent all night. When we spoke, it was to tell stories.

A midwife, mother of four, began. "My mother warned me about wantonness by telling me about Grandmother Amanda. She's my namesake, and we both share the same birthday. There's a portrait of her that I inherited—a young woman in white robes clings to a granite cross, wild waves everywhere, and the inscription: 'Our Dear Mother, Amanda, 1906, 30 years, 4 months, 4 days.'"

We were all quiet, candles glowing as if in memoriam these many years later. Above us, through the tepeelike opening, shone a full June Moon. There was the sweet smell of honeysuckle mixed with the medicinal scent of mugwort and other herbs we used for pain, for cleansing.

The midwife's face was dark, indistinct. I remember her hands, slender and strong. These were hands that welcomed newborns and stroked a mother's back bent in labor. For fifteen years this midwife had greeted over 500 babies. Now, she continued, "My Grandmother Amanda died of an abortion. She was thirty and had five children already. When her husband found Grandmother Amanda bleeding, he called the doctor, who rode out on his horse. But when the doctor recognized the abortive wound, he turned on his heels and walked away. 'She deserves it,' he told my grandfather. 'It's God's punishment for what she's done.'"

The midwife was still, then at last continued. "As a child, I felt haunted by my grandma Amanda. That picture of her hanging on a cross ... that '4 months, 4 days' ... I thought it was a code for how long she'd been pregnant. Later, when I traveled to Japan for my own illegal abortion, I sat in that strange hotel, holding pillows to my belly and sobbing. I imagined I talked to my unborn child and to Grandmother Amanda. I rocked and rocked. All night after the abortion, my older sister sat with me and held me as I bent double over those pillows. I was fifteen, and I understood everything."

Power in the blood—power and terrible knowledge. The knowledge of life and death and responsibility. As I sat listening, I realized these stories weren't the "old wives' tales" we've been warned against. They were old wise tales of women who, like the Great Mother, made the most profound choice we humans have—to give and to take life. This birth-death wisdom is born of woman, even in the Old Testament. For Eve is the first to taste of the Tree of Knowledge. And from this ancient, serpent-inspired knowledge comes mortality. It is as if the Hebrew God had to acknowledge and then punish the women for their encompassing both life and death.

The image of a woman hanging on a cross, a bloody woman at that, is blasphemous to a believer in the Old Testament God. But to those who call themselves Christian, it can also symbolize Christ's sacrifice so that we might be rebirthed. Christ's function in the New Testament is feminine: to reenact the blood rites, the cycle of birth, death, and rebirth. For without blood there cannot be birth—this much of our human biology survived the Old Testament censorship.

Those women who follow an Old Testament God have not yet integrated the feminine Christ. They are stuck not in a cycle of birth, death, and rebirth but in death. Every time these women contemplate the act of abortion, they see it as a separate, unrelated act of female (therefore unsanctioned) judgment. The religion under which these women labor is based on an Old Testament in which Christ is all potential, *unborn*. To the pro-life mind, it is the blood of this unborn, wounded Messiah-child, instead of the female body's natural blood, that is shed every time a woman chooses abortion. Every time pro-life women speak of their rights, what gets translated through this Old Testament myth is only the right to kill the unborn. Thus, sacrificial death is not linked by a healing feminine cycle to rebirth. This lifelong mothering cycle is irrelevant to a religion riveted on the death myth of crucifixion.

To the pro-life fundamentalists, the ultimate drama is not played out in picket lines or even courts. It takes place in the spiritual passion play of the Devil versus God. Because the drama, like Jehovah, is outside and beyond us, the focus on earthly matters is of scant importance. Perhaps this is why my sister and her sisterhood are not radicalized by social reform issues. My sister is much less interested in nuclear disarmament, the environment, or unemployment. In fact, she favors capital punishment; it is killing of one judged by *logos,* or the law of God the Father. The one punished by death is judged as "not innocent."

Innocence, for fundamentalists, is lost at birth. Once you're born, you're bad. Bad as the Earth herself after the Fall. In medieval paintings, the world was depicted as the Devil's excrement. Into this dung pile comes the spiritually pure child—God's divine seed. Throughout the Middle Ages and into the Renaissance, it was believed that every drop of male semen contained a miniature, unseen fetus. The woman was God's vessel, to hold His holy seed until it was born. As passive receptacle, the woman's body, like the Earth, was meant to be abandoned, transcended, shed—the way a spiritual seedling must shatter and cast off its worthless shell. Not until 1827, with the scientific discovery of the ovum, was this myth of male seed as the divine source of all life itself shattered. It became biologically obvious that the female had her equal share of divine spark.

But society always lags behind science. Today, a woman's body is still not seen as divine or sacred unless she is pregnant, a dwelling place for the holy male seed. Once the woman's body is emptied of the fetus, that potential Christ-child, the woman returns to her natural state, which, like that of the Earth, is of the Devil. The part of the woman's body that is not of the Devil is her womb. A womb is invisible, a spiritual temple within which a man can worship because it holds and nurtures the seed that will perpetuate him, his name. If, during this blessed gestation, a fetus has its separate soul, does that soul also need God's forgiveness for being human? Why does the Catholic church baptize a baby at birth and not at conception?

I suspect there is an official Catholic dictum to answer this question, though my Catholic friends cannot find answers in their catechism. In fact, it was Pope Innocent XI who in 1679 overturned a ban on abortion, allowing it before "quickening" (when the fetus is first felt by the mother) and stating that abortion is not murder because "the fetus lacks a rational soul and begins first to have one when it is born." And St. Thomas Aquinas, the thirteenth-century thinker, pinpointed "ensoulment"—the moment a fetus becomes human—at exactly forty days after conception for males and eighty days after conception for females. The longer gestation of a female soul says volumes about the church's meager estimation of women. But the more unusual point of these papal and patriarchal pronouncements is that fetal gestation was not then the battleground it is today.

Perhaps gestation is spared many of the church's rituals of sin and redemption because it is still perceived as a biological Garden of Eden. It is possible then that pro-life women see the decision to abort as a reenactment of the Fall? For into this gestative Garden enters the snake. In pre-Christian cultures, the snake symbolized feminine wisdom. It is this snake who counsels a woman to exercise her Great Mother power of giving death, as well as life. Ancient depictions of the Goddess show her encircled with snakes like resplendent bracelets. And there are some archaeologists who speculate that the original Garden of Eden existed in the peaceful centuries of Goddess culture.

In our culture, still dominated by the masculine myth of war, the act of killing presupposes an enemy. In the older cultures, the taking of an unborn child's life, like Christ's crucifixion, was seen as a sacrifice, which in its original Latin means "to make sacred." As French scholar Ginette Paris observes in *Pagan Meditations:* "One aborts an impossible love, not a hatred." Primitive tribeswomen today still speak to the spirits of their unborn children before performing their ritual abortions. After the act, the woman is received by her tribal sisters and comforted in her grief, her loss, her choice.

As I sat in that moon lodge this summer, I wondered what might have happened if my own sister had walked out of her abortion clinic into the wide arms of a society of women welcoming her to the hard mysteries of life and death. What if nowadays the tribes of women outside abortion clinics were there not to bar entrance but rather to comfort and acknowledge a feminine sacrament? What if women's clinics were not based only on the masculine medical model of disease and surgical procedure but also on feminine healing? Why not a moon lodge near every abortion clinic, where a tribe of women meditate and comfort their own in the darkest phase of a woman's moon? My own sister is still comfortless these many years after her abortion. Perhaps she simply sought the first tribe of women she could find who were focused on abortion. And how terrible that her solace is to continually tell and live the story of her repented sin.

It is interesting to note here that nowhere in the Old Testament does Jehovah actually forbid abortion, as He so specifically does acts such as false worship, adultery, and lying. Jehovah concerns Himself more with rules for masculine sexuality. He punishes Onan with death for spilling his seed on the Earth to prevent his brother's wife from conceiving. The prohibition against onanism, or male masturbation, which wastes God's seed, was the theological base for many of the later laws against contraception, homosexuality, and abortion.

The Old Testament myth is still very much with us. In 1988, *Newsweek* reported that one out of every six women in this country who has an abortion describes herself as an "evangelical Christian." And throughout the developing world, where American aid for family planning evangelically extends our fundamentalist stigma against abortion, a woman dies from a self-inflicted abortion every three minutes.

If it is only God the Father who "giveth and taketh away," if it is only God the Father who can sacrifice His own child because "God so loved the world"; if it is only God the Father who can sacrifice and redeem a child— then what can God the Mother do? She can give birth, and she can sacrifice herself for her child.

That summer night as I sat in the moon lodge, I longed for my little sister. But she would never accompany me to that red hut of women. Still, there might be some common ground.

"Sometimes the smallest things can bring us together," a younger woman in our moon lodge commented. "Like the women I work with. There's five of us in a department headed by a man. Well, we women aren't all close friends, but somehow we pretty much always know when we each start our periods. And because our boss would be embarrassed by such women's talk and we work in an open office, one of us came up with a rather subversive idea: On the first day of her period, she'd wear her elegant little Moon necklace. That gave me the idea of putting my favorite Picasso postcard—you know, the Cubist style of that woman's face split in half and kind of weird, wacked out?—up on my desk to let everyone know: *Back off!* Soon every one of us had a talisman for her moon time. Another co-worker always wore her red silk blouse; another woman bought herself flowers for her desk. She told our boss they were from her boyfriend. Do you think he ever noticed that those flowers came every month on the full Moon? We wondered, because without any word from us and probably without knowing what hit him, that guy went out and bought himself a watch with the phases of the Moon on it. Very expensive, that watch. But considering the money we saved him, by acknowledging and working within our natural rhythms, it might have been a bargain!"

In the moon lodge we all laughed, listening to crickets down by the lake. Bull frogs chimed in with their sonorous seesaw chorus. The Moon gleaming into our hut was so bright that someone asked, "Anyone know Moon stories?"

The midwife told us first of Artemis/Diana, goddess of wisdom, the hunt, the Moon, and childbirth. Her mother, Leto, gave birth to Zeus's twins—Artemis and Apollo. Artemis's birth was completely painless; she turned and midwifed her mother during Apollo's dangerous, difficult birth. It was to Artemis, the midwife told us, that women cried out in childbirth pain or ecstasy. As goddess of the hunt, Artemis also sacrificed the animals she loved—and this destructive element in her nature was in perfect sync with her role as bringer of children into the world.

As the midwife told more stories of feminine deities—the gnostic Sophia, who, like the Egyptian Isis and Babylonian Ishtar/Inanna descended to the underworld to find wisdom and rebirth (and often to save her masculine counterpart), the Chinese Buddhist Kuan Yin, all-compassionate and wise—I remembered my great-grandmother's wedding ring. It is mine now—this antique, very delicate cameo of Artemis. My great-grandfather had it made for my great-grandmother to honor her hunting skill. She attracted his devotion after taking first prize in a turkey shoot. He lost the shoot but gained a wife. I remember this great-grandmother well; she was shrewd yet kind. She would not hunt bears, once the animal totem of Artemis. It is from the word *bear* that we take the phrase "to bear" children, surely an Artemisian task.

But it occurred to me, thinking of my great-grandmother whose ring is my heirloom, that she did not pass down to her daughter the feminine secrets of birth, death, fertility. The goddess of the hunt, a masculine myth, survived proudly in my family's storytelling. But what became of Artemis's midwifery and feminine secrets?

About the time my great-grandmother was accepting her Artemis wedding ring, the role of women as midwives was becoming increasingly unacceptable. Up until the mid-1800s, abortion in this country was legal. The movement to stop the midwives and "granny women" or "yarb doctors," as they were called in the South, was spearheaded by a fledgling American Medical Association campaigning against abortion practitioners. The tradition of midwives was economically competitive, not to mention undermining to a doctor's authority. Again, we have a male priesthood repressing women's traditional societies and secrets in true Old Testament style.

A God who will have no others before Him. A God who does not share and, in fact, steals power from the feminine. A God without a partner. What does this God do with daughters? He declares war on the Devil through their bodies, and the women, in turn, declare war on themselves, their sisters.

But what if, instead of warring with our sisters, women found another way?

"I would like to dedicate this moon lodge in the name of my two sisters, my great-grandmother, hunter and mid-wife, and my own mother," I said to the other women surrounding me. It was almost light. We were luxuriously sleepy; there was much blood shed among us. And with all the squatting, storytelling, and herbs, our cramps were gone. What was left was a trancelike contentment—for we'd shared a rite of passage long overdue us.

We turned to the midwife to lead us in an old chant:

I am the daughter of the ancient Mother
I am the daughter of the Mother of the world.
O Inanna, O Inanna
It is you who teaches us
To die, be reborn, and rise again.

Then she said, "There are so many stories we could tell that women have told for thousands of years."

She reminded us of the Eleusinian mysteries of Demeter and Persephone. For centuries those mystery religions gave ancients hope of rebirth by participating in Mother Demeter's search to reunite with her daughter Persephone, queen of the Underworld, who brings the new life of spring back to a barren winter world. Another woman sang a chant to Isis, who helps us heal by lovingly re-membering her dismembered masculine mate, Osiris. An older woman, a professor, invoked *gnosis kardias*, the "way of the knowing heart," by calling on Sophia. At last the youngest woman told this recent story: On the day the first man walked on the Moon, a woman archaeologist discovered the ancient, lost Temple of Aphrodite, goddess of love and the Moon. Dolphins accompanied that archaeologist to the buried site in Turkey. Her story didn't make the newspapers, of course, for many years. It was a man's conquest of the Moon, not a woman's rediscovery of reverence for that Moon, that made headlines. "But rediscovery never belongs to the past," the young woman said firmly. "It belongs to the present and the future. It's what we make of it, once we discover it again."

At dawn we decided to tell a last story, the Navajo

myth of Spider Grandmother. She is the smallest of the small, the greatest of the great. It was seemingly unimportant Spider Grandmother who brought light to her people after all the warriors had failed to capture the Sun. Spider Grandmother simply spun a small web to carry a bit of the Sun back to her tribe. I believe that night in our moon lodge we five women telling our small stories spun a web to bring some Moon light back to our own little tribes.

"Know the male," instructs the illustrious *Tao Te Ching*, "but keep to the female." For thousands of years, women and men have earnestly apprenticed themselves to "know the male." But many women have discovered that this is not the same as the Delphic oracle "Know thyself." Delphi takes its name from the Greek word *delphe*, or "womb [of the earth]"—also "dolphin," or *Delphinus delphis*. Long before Delphi was Apollo's sacred oracle, it was dedicated to Gaia, Mother Earth. The oracular prophecies were always delivered by women to men and women alike until the oracle was at last destroyed by a Christian emperor. This most famous Delphic wisdom of knowing ourselves, means that we all, male and female, must know our own feminine mysteries, and our Earth.

That night in the moon lodge, I learned something about myself that had always mystified me. My moon, my first blood, began on the day of our school's big 6,000-yard walk-run. When I ran that dreaded race, I suddenly had so much power, I flew around the track. Never before or since have I won any footrace. And why, on the original day of menstruation? That night in the moon lodge, I learned that Changing Woman, called White Bead Woman, on her holy day of first menstruation, also

ran a race. That is why the Navajos call a girl's first menstruation her "first race." She is given gifts because she
has passed a threshold into her own power and mystery.
Since that moon lodge night, I've made it a practice to
buy myself a gift on the first day of my monthly moon—a
small, and now not always private celebration.

I would like to give my sister a gift, too. But I must give
her something she can accept. She cannot accept women
in moon lodges. She has her own myth to live by. What I
can give my sister is something that I cannot buy. It is a
gift exchange more difficult because it requires that I sus-
pend my own beliefs and try to understand, if not
embrace hers. What can I give my sister, then, in this
attempt at understanding?

In unraveling the myth that motivates her pro-life
advocacy, I must acknowledge and allow my sister her
very real pain about my own belief in legalized abortion.
I must understand that I have no control over her projec-
tion that I am a potential murderer. My sister's
vengeance against abortion is savage because hers is a
savage God. Perhaps their vendetta gives my sister and
the other pro-life women a respite from a God ever-vigi-
lant and cognizant of their original sin. First of all, she is
a woman—the Eve who supposedly is the root of all evil.
Second, she has killed her child. Is it any wonder she par-
ticipates in the only saving grace left her: to keep other
women from her own fate, her fatal mistake, her feminin-
ity, her Fall?

The mistake pro-choice advocates make is engaging in
this passion play or self-proclaimed holy war from a
defensive or offensive posture. Instead, we might stand

back from the fray and gaze upon this Warrior God–inspired movement as if it were simply the last gasp of patriarchal Christianity. This does not mean that we will refrain from legal lobbying in behalf of choice; it means simply that we must *not* engage in the warfare mentality against our sisters. It means gazing at them across the picket lines with compassion and nonviolent *gnosis*. We must act not from the fear and anger that belong to the old masculine testament but from our own feminine, knowing hearts. This understanding is a right that can never be lost or legalized.

Some of us who are pro-choice are in much the same situation as conscientious objectors were during the world wars. Nor do we want to counter these fundamentalists with an evangelicalism of our own. Fear, anger, and self-righteousness make zealots, and even Christ refused to be a zealot. Warrior ways and thinking lead to battle.

How can I declare war on my own sister? She is not my enemy. She is my own blood. And blood is sacred. If I engage only on the level of exchange offered me—war, the masculine way of wounding to reach that sacred and powerful blood—my sister and I will dehumanize each other so terribly that we'll forget we are from the same family.

What about finally finding the feminine way of power to balance our masculine ritual of *logos* (i.e., court trials, the flesh or word made legislation)? What about remembering that a woman's bloodletting can be natural, in keeping with the Earth's cycle? And finally, what about holding up to those driven by the Old Testament God the balance of a Christ who offered the seemingly impossible "Love your enemies"?

In this last decade of the millennia, we find ourselves in this country eerily without enemies. The Cold War has ended and we are now declared allies of a Russia struggling toward democracy. Pulling back from the "one-minute-to-midnight" scenario of nuclear war, our superpower countries are offered the challenge of another myth—one without enemies, one based not on dominion but on necessary balance and partnership so that we might survive. No wonder that we are looking back to research a little-known period in our species' history that was peaceful and cooperative, in harmony with our natural world. And no wonder that, as we change our personal and collective myth from war to mutual survival, there is this backlash of those whose religion is centered on a male, warrior God.

The glory of war and death must be evolved into the glory of living. I propose to pitch my moon lodge a distance from all the battle in this war of the women. There I'll share stories with my sisters rather than attack or defend myself from them. Running across the lines our daughters could be bearing gifts on the first days of our moons, no matter our politics. With my small society of friends, I'll continue to chart our reproductive rhythms, a way of keeping time that is again timely. Knowing my body's temperature and reproductive cycle is a right no one can take away from me. And I'll continue to explore the feminine myths that have everyday meaning for me and my tribe. There are also teachings in every spiritual tradition, from Chinese Taoism to American Indian, celebrating sexual mysteries of conscious creation. There are women's secret societies that teach traditional remedies, herbs, rituals, and meditations to control and increase fertility. All these feminine ways of knowing ourselves may well be invaluable in a world bent on restricting our modern medical abortion procedures. There is so much to remember, to put back together of this feminine that has been so fragmented and forgotten.

If I had a daughter, when it came time to celebrate her rite of feminine passage, I would offer to take her to a moon lodge. There, in the company of witnessing women, we'd tell our stories and old wise tales of what it is to embody the blood and power of the feminine. No matter what the laws dictate, no matter how the abortion war might rage, there will also be these private nights of tribal, feminine knowing. There will be moon lodges pitched beyond the battlefields. Within them we will welcome and remember and give rebirth to an old and new myth. And there, we can teach our daughters, while the Moon shines on their brave womanliness, a meditation on the rite of abortion that was made the night of my first moon lodge:

> I am practicing this ritual feminine sacrifice of sacred blood for all my ancestors, for my women's tribe to honor a still, small voice. I take part in this death rite that ends in rebirth. I know what I do is sorrowful, and I seek succor, from my own soul and others. I ask the Great Mother and the Great Father to be near me, to comfort and hold me in arms that so love me and my world. I commit this responsible act because I believe the world, not the womb, is the true Garden. Because I believe birth is a celebration, not a damnation. It is a time of original orgasm, not original sin. And when I do give birth, it will be done with much wisdom and life-long mothering. I now ask for the spirit of this, my

child, to come again when the world and when I will welcome its rebirth.

If my own mother had remembered what her great-grandmother knew of the Artemisian herbs and midwife practices, I might not have been born. I think about that shadow these days, as the war of the women escalates. I know my mother's despair, and I know my own. My mother is every woman who, no matter the laws, will make this soul-searching, mortal choice; and I am every child waiting to be truly welcomed into the world.

My own birth was met with sadness and dismay. To be unwelcome is to spend much of one's life seeking that wide, feminine embrace of the Great Mother in a family and a culture that forsakes the feminine. If the Great Father will have no other gods before Him, why not a Great Mother beside to balance Him?

It was the women who took Christ down off that cross. Spirit may have abandoned His broken body, but the women did not. In a small, unheroic act, they carried Christ like a child back to the Earth's womb, back to the Great Mother, to be born again. It was to Mary Magdalene, His earthly companion, that Christ first chose to reveal his resurrection.

Can we now, these thousands of years later, allow ourselves, like Christ, to receive the forgiving embrace of the feminine? Then we can take ourselves down off that old, rugged cross and accept the strong, balancing arms of God the Mother—She, who also gives and takes life, She who calls our fundamentalist sisters back from their Old Testament fall, into their knowing hearts, their full, fearless power.

# SISTERS OF THE ROAD

My aunts are a wild lot. Ozark born and backwoods bred, Aunts Nettie Mae, Mary Leola, and Donna Ruth explain their electric spirits by saying, "We got a touch of the tarbrush and a touch of the tepee in our blood. That makes our family just plain touched."

Most summers of my childhood were spent in the wayward company of these aunts, who provided a perfect counterpoint to my father's (their brother's) pretense of normalcy and practical calm. "Cutups," my aunts called themselves. To this day it is their greatest delight to aim potshots, if not punches, at the "balloon heads that pass for menfolk in our family."

This summer, at a biyearly family reunion in northern Georgia, hosted by Aunt Mary Leola, my aunts pushed my father into the motel swimming pool right in the middle of one of his "lecture series," as Nettie Mae dryly describes my father's penchant for impromptu pontificating.

"Listen to your daddy, you gals," she mugged behind his back, before shoving him unceremoniously into the water. "He's the world's expert on everything!"

If there were any experts in my family's tribe, they were my rambunctious aunts. Like imprinted ducklings, my two sisters and I used to tag after our aunts—smoking as they did in the piny woods, dancing to the 1950s bebop, and defying my parents' stern religion with so much laughter that we were lamented by my mother as "born-again backslid."

Our aunts not only tolerated my sisters' and my gawky devotion, they embraced it. "We never had no time or money for no doll babies," Aunt Mary Leola explained in her deep, tobacco-rough voice. "You young'uns were our toys. We got some of our childhood back when we played with you gals."

My aunts' and father's childhood was marked by poverty, not play. Nettie Mae tells the story of the one pair of shoes she and my father shared; they went to school on alternate days, depending on whose turn it was to wear the shoes and walk the ten miles to a country schoolhouse. Nevertheless, my father won the state spelling bee when he was in third grade, and Nettie Mae was known for her shrewdness at numbers and reading. The oldest of the five farm children, Nettie Mae was married young to a full-blooded Cherokee who, as Donna Ruth likes to say, "adores her so much, Nettie Mae might as well be his whole tribe."

As children, my sisters and I were afraid of this taciturn Uncle George; his humor was black and beyond us. Now, he's a favorite uncle, a man to be counted on to demonstrate how to treat a lady. Last reunion, we sat spellbound as Uncle George packed Nettie Mae's suitcase, his masculine paws perfectly folding our aunt's negligee like holy raiment. We'd always seen my mother packing my father's suitcase for his frequent business trips. But Uncle George's tenderness with his wife's underwear, the exact way he folded the pleats in her pedal pushers, the bright cotton socks he handled so deftly, as if juggling warm popovers—we realized that none of our boyfriends and husbands had ever folded our laundry, much less packed our suitcases.

"It's a revelation to these gals, Nettie Mae," Donna Ruth joked and poked her husband's ribs. "Now, my Bill here, I have to stay on top of him every minute or he might turn right back into a male chauvinist pig!"

"Suuuu-weeee ...," my aunts yodeled in unison.

Donna Ruth's fifth husband, Bill, is a Lutheran minister whose sense of humor matches his wife's. "How else would I survive these sisters of hers?" He laughs. "A man either laughs with them or they're on off down the road."

Off down the road might well be a one-way trip cross-country. There is a tradition in my father's family of criss-crossing the continent in family caravans, like reunions on the road. To travel with my aunts and all my cousins was to be part of a chain of vans, pickups, and U-Hauls that stopped and circled at night in a wagon train of family. We still take over entire motels. When Grandaddy died, all fifty of us piled into an Ozark motel. After crying our eyes out for two days, we decided to play practical jokes on one another—hiding cars, dousing one another from balconies with water balloons, and generally raising hell by way of a wake. My sister remarked that we'd done Grandaddy proud because we "figured out how to put the *fun* back into funeral."

After the funeral, caravans took over every which way. My sisters and I, along with Cousin Doug, continued our road reunion through the South—from the Ozarks to Memphis to Atlanta to Miami.

It was Cousin Doug who gave us the supreme compliment. "You girls have taken over where our aunts left off."

He was referring to the "rebels-of-the-road" way we sisters now travel, a direct inheritance from Nettie Mae, Donna Ruth, and Mary Leola. It isn't that we're so openminded. My younger sister—whom we call Marla Mosby after Colonel John S. Mosby, the Confederate Gray Ghost who terrorized Yankees—is "wild in the wrong direction," as my sister Paula ("Pooh") gleefully explains. Riding in Mosby's van, complete with shag rug and VCR in the back for her three boys, was for me like riding around inside my political opponent's point of view. As we tooled past Graceland, the great Elvis's mansion near Memphis, other drivers shook their fists at me when they passed, truck drivers honked their horns as if in hearty agreement, and several otherwise ordinary women screamed obscenities at me behind the wheel. It was only when we stopped for one of our favorite backwoods barbecue road stops that I noticed Mosby's bumper sticker: IF YOU CAN READ THIS, THANK THE DOCTOR WHO DIDN'T ABORT YOU!

Last summer's family reunion saw yet another series of sisters on the road. The moment I arrived in north Georgia, Aunts Mary Leola and Donna Ruth swept me up between them for a ride into the backcountry in Mary Leola's red pickup truck. Her husband, Lloyd, had recently died, leaving Mary not much more than her sixty-two infertile acres and farmhouse. All four of her children live within fifteen minutes' drive of Mary Leola, and they share tending to their mother's land and needs. Mary Leola raises peacocks "so stupid I had to buy me some little roosters to teach 'em not to fall into their drinking water and eat their food instead of stare at it while starving." She also has a day job, which "runs her ragged."

Sitting between my aunts as we roared over red ruts in the Georgia backwoods, Mary Leola smoking Pall Malls and Donna Ruth telling family jokes, I couldn't help but notice the gearshift grinding between my thighs.

"Aunt Mary," I protested, "can't you shift without goosing me?"

"Ahhhh, honey." She howled. "You've had worse!"

At that my aunts screamed with laughter and almost missed stopping for a garage sale at which I bought a tape recorder for five bucks and Aunt Mary Leola bought me a hand-crocheted, button-on red-yarn collar. I also bought my father a birthday belt buckle with a broncing buck on it for three dollars, and Donna Ruth purchased a country wildflower porcelain vase. Then it was back on the road, radio blaring country and western as we three sang along at the top of our voices.

My brother-in-law Lance calls our multigenerational sisters-of-the-road legacy "Talk and Ride." "All you women do is talk and ride and sing," he complained on the few short trips he shared with my aunts or my sisters and me. My aunts also found a way to push Lance into the pool. A day later he was blithely pushed down a hill, video camera equipment banging all the way, to remind him that "only men who really *like* women are allowed here." As a final ritual, Aunt Mary Leola smeared chocolate frosting all over Lance's face when he was found guilty of uttering a sexist statement. He fought back by dropping a pincer bug down Mary's "front porch," as she calls her ample bosom.

On my CPA cousin Little Lloyd's wooden front porch the day my sisters and I took off for our road trip through Georgia to the Florida Keys, Mary Leola settled next to me on the swing, and we rocked in the midday heat. Aunt Mary detailed for me the secret recipe for her beloved blackberry cobbler, then settled back in the swing, lit a cigarette, thoughtfully picked a slit of tobacco from her lip, and took up what we call her "storytelling song." Her deep voice dropped into a lulling, melodic chant.

"Brenda Sue, little sister, you see that house over yonder?"

"Yes'm."

"Use the family feeling and see what you git offn' that old place."

I closed my eyes and tuned in to the family ESP we all struggle to understand as another kind of evidence to be weighed with all the rest. "Well ... violence and passion ... maybe murder. Something feels real bad over there ..."

"Yes, indeed," Aunt Mary took up, nodding. For a moment it was as if we'd both fallen asleep in a wooden cradle that creaked and swung and stirred the only breeze. "Little Lloyd's wife's brother, Rayon, was livin' there. He had this little gal come up right regular. They was real cozy until she stopped comin' round. Then one day, Little Lloyd sees her truck, figures they's done made up." Aunt Mary gave me a deep look. Her black eyes are hooded, her cheekbones high, her skin swarthy with the Seminole blood running strong in her veins. My immediate family are the only ones who don't show the Indian blood. "White people," the others call us; we've always felt somewhat ashamed of our fair skin, how we six stand out like a bright knot amidst dark, handsome faces in reunion photos.

"What'dya think happens next, darlin'?" Aunt Mary Leola fixed me with her ancient Indian eyes. It's what she's asked me all my life, as if the story were already told and we simply had to remember it, tap into its rhythms and rightness like tributaries finding their main stream.

"Someone dies."

"Oh, honey." Mary Leola nodded. "You *are* with me." She lit another cigarette, and smoke hung in the air like humidity. "Well, Little Lloyd decides after three days of not seeing hide nor hair of anybody—not Rayon, not his girlfriend—to investigate. Little Lloyd walks into the house, helloing his head off. No answer. Sudden, he sees blood smeared everywhere—on the walls, on the TV set, the phone with its wires cut clean through. He starts in to shaking, but he's brave and goes deeper into that bloody house. There on the linoleum kitchen floor he finds Rayon's little gal, lyin' flat and still. Lordy, that gal's got three eyes ... and the one in the middle is a bullet hole!"

The swing stopped, and Mary Leola stared straight at me. "Young'un, she'd been alyin' there three days and three nights just like sweet Jesus in the tomb."

"Did she live?" I demanded.

"Wouldn't call it no resurrection." Mary Leola sighed.

"Sure, she's walkin' round now, draggin' an arm and a leg. Says she's got no memory a'tall of that night. I think she's just scared witless. Wouldn't you be? And Little Lloyd like to crack up at the sight of that gal shot smack between the eyes. Put him off his accounting numbers for some weeks. Then they done found that boy Rayon ten days later. He was the major suspect until a fisherman seen him layin' up in the crick back yonder. Rayon was so disintegrated, there weren't nothin' left of him but a high school ring." Aunt Mary Leola turns to me, a hand slung around my shoulder. "Ain't that a mystery now? You tell *me* what happened, child."

I tried. I made up plots and subplots, and we swung higher until my sisters called me away.

We piled each set of their kids into two identical vans, revved for our continuing cross-country reunion.

"Y'all finish the story in the car, honey" is how Mary Leola says good-bye. "Carry my love along. Precious cargo." As we embraced, she added softly, "You take care your sisters, hear? We ain't gonna have no nursing homes in this family. We're gonna set up our own. Women outlast their men, that's a fact. And nowadays old people got more siblings than children to take care of them. Nettie Mae, Donna Ruth, and I got it all planned. We done raised one another ... hell, who else can bury us proper?"

As my sisters, Pooh and Mosby, and I drove off, we weren't three miles out of town before we were on the CBs that make our Talk and Ride easy between vans. We sisters have our own frequency, tuned beneath the truckers with their dull delight in spotting Smokeys and good peach pie pit stops. On our CB frequency, we don't exchange facts; we take up our stories. As Pooh says, "Gossip is our path to the soul."

"What do you think of Aunt Mary's idea?" I asked Pooh in the lead car. Her handle is Pink Pistol. Mine is Rambling Ruby. "Want to all of us live together when we're old?"

"Sure thing, Ramble!" Pooh's voice crackled. "But I'm not going to cook anymore. We'll hire help, play killer Ping-Pong instead of shuffleboard, and we'll dance instead of do that stupid low-impact aerobics for ancients."

Mosby, riding shotgun with the Pink Pistol, took over the CB. "Roger, this is Gray Ghost ..." Behind her three children screamed to take their turn, and there were signs of a struggle over the microphone. Her sovereignty at last restored to the airwaves, Mosby said, "You know, I was working in this nursing home with these two old ladies, Miss Eula and Miss Louise. They'd never left Virginia in their ninety-odd years. Sisters, they were. I overheard Miss Eula tell Miss Louise that their new doctor was no gentleman because he didn't wear his shirttail tucked in. Thing is, the poor guy was wearing scrubs! Anyway, Miss Eula said she guessed she had to forgive him because he was from Ethiopia. When Miss Louise asked, 'Where's Eeeetheeeoooopeeea?' Miss Eula said, 'Oh, honey, it's somewhere south there of Richmond.'"

"We won't make that mistake," I said. "Not with all our traveling."

"Not unless one of us is senile!" the Pink Pistol shouted into the CB.

"Hey, Ramble, you believe in euthanasia?"

"For my sisters, yes," I teased. "It might be self-defense if we all end up living together again."

The CB fell silent, static companionably crackling between the cars. Someone turned on the VCR behind my driver's seat, watching *The Little Mermaid* for the hundredth time. I look around at my two nieces and a nephew, who sang along with "Kiss the Girl"—every word perfect. One was learning harmony from listening to her mother and aunts on this caravan.

The night before I had told my nephews and nieces the continuing story we were all making up called "Bandito Bear." The youngest of three girls, Lissie, sobbed upon hearing that Bandito's great grizzly mother had died and left him starving. "Didn't Bandito Bear have *sistuhs?*" she wailed with her southern accent, unable to imagine life without a sister-caretaker.

Fierce sisterhood, the habit of rebellion and true believers, runs strong in my family. Both of my grandmothers taught college during World War I, only to be replaced by men returning from war. One grandmother fell from the intellectual grace of teaching university astronomy courses to teaching kindergarten; the other descended deep into madness. But each passed along to her daughters a highly charged current of brilliance short-circuited. The next generation tenaciously took up the grandmothers' dropped torch and burned bright; my aunts formed their own feminine family to support their declared matriarchy. While marrying, they kept their compass on the True North of feminine rights and realms. I have never seen any of my aunts "kowtow to any man," as they'd put it. Nor have I seen them reverse the roles and "ride roughshod" over their men. They have simply let their husbands know that "I got sisters watching over me—and you." This last is said sweetly but with that inherited undercurrent that is so electric it is almost audible, the hiss of a snake, the sizzle of live wires.

There is a history in my family of sisters running away together. My aunts have all lived with one another when marriages went awry. Their future sisters' nursing home seems as pragmatic and shrewd as any other retirement plan. My mother didn't have sisters but quickly took up her in-laws' ways. She made a habit of running off to Southern Baptist conventions with her Women's Missionary Union sisters. In the early sixties, when women did not have the vote in her church, my mother and comrades commandeered the floor of the great convention hall in Virginia Beach and filibustered with all their feminine fury until the members allowed as women should be able to vote in their own churches.

My own sisters and I travel together at least once a year—and often we have planned these trips to heal broken hearts and homes. My brothers-in-law joke that these sisters-of-the-road leave-takings have warded off any divorces so far among my siblings. But, as Pooh coolly remarks, "We've practiced leaving our husbands so many times, they know we mean business." Again, that slight crackling in the air.

The feminine electricity is like static on our sister CBs as we move down the highway. On this latest summer's sojourn, there was a deeper journey we three sisters took together. For the past decade my middle sister, Pooh, and I have been quietly aghast, guiltily united in our despair over our youngest sister, Mosby's, zealous anti-abortion campaigns. Mosby was always marching on DC or wherever her adopted right-to-life sisters were pitching their next battle. Pooh, ever the mediator in our sibling bond, took the tack of listening to Mosby's rants and engaging with the Gray Ghost in political skirmishes. I, the eldest, simply dropped out of the dialogue and kept to the more tender track, mothering Mosby in the hope that she might feel our bond was deeper than our opposite beliefs. Of the two tactics, I must say Pooh's worked better over the years. Because she and Mosby were always in the fray, they were in constant communication. My benign distance increased into private dismay whenever Mosby would be arrested trying to block young women from entering an abortion clinic. Unlike my weekly communion with Pooh on the phone, my intimacy with Mosby fell into ritual patterns—holidays, birthdays, emergencies.

So this summer's reunion, with all three sisters and children traveling South together, loomed as a potential disaster. As I climbed into Mosby's van, I noted her new bumper stickers, one reflecting her patriotism over the Persian Gulf, the other a modified version of her anti-abortion stand. SUPPORT OUR TROOPS declared the left side of her bumper; and, on the right, ABORTION STOPS A BEATING HEART was inscribed over the bright red medical zigzags of an EKG chart. My nephews happily informed me that they'd named their dog Patriot after the successful Patriot missile system; and my youngest nephew wore his Persian Gulf T-shirt on the trip. Since it was the Fourth of July, we stopped for fireworks in Stone Mountain, Georgia, where a laser program was beamed against the granite monolith carving of Jefferson Davis, Stonewall Jackson, and General Robert E. Lee. As a country singer intoned "Glory, glory, hallelujah" from "The Battle Hymn of the Republic," the fundamentalists and patriots in my family snapped to attention while I sat quietly eyeing fireflies. In the dark our phosphorescent headbands glowed orange and purple like halos.

"This must be hell on a liberal like you, sis!" My sister Mosby leaned over and laughed. "Don't think you're the ugly-duckling misfit, darling. You do belong in this family. We'd never let you go."

I don't ever want to be let go—as strange as my family is, as wild as my aunts are, as different as I am from my siblings, we grew from common ground. Later on down the road, as I was riding with Mosby, she turned to me and said softly, "Remember all those summer nights down on the Yellow River when we used to live here in Georgia? You and I sitting on the riverbanks, with our feet in the water and talking. I was in high school, you were home from college, and we told each other everything. We'd just moved and I was a mess. Daddy told you if you didn't make all of us happy, he wouldn't send you back to California to finish school. You thought you were going crazy with dizzy spells, and the doctors said it might be a brain tumor ..."

"Oh, those were the days ..." I made a face.

"It was a nightmare, sure" She fell silent. "But we could talk about it; we told each other we were wide awake in the middle of a bad dream. I thought if we could be close then, we'd get through anything."

"We have," I said. "We will."

"Politics ain't nothing compared to a nightmare," Mosby said.

We looked steadily at each other, she now in the driver's seat and me handing out pimento cheese sandwiches our aunts had packed us for the trip. Behind us, the children fought over their food. "I've still got my beliefs," Mosby said softly, "*and* my sisters."

There was that subtle electricity, then static on the CB as the Pink Pistol tuned in from her lead car. "Any y'all feel like a pit stop? There's peach cobbler down the road at Exit 212. Aunt Mary's cobbler didn't last a minute with these savages."

"Suuu-weeeee," we all sang between cars, between the seats, the states. "Sisters of the road!"

We continued on like that all the way to one of our homes. Just last week Mosby called to say she was bound to Wichita, Kansas, to "check out" the anti-abortion action since the latest court ruling that many now either hope or fear will soon repeal *Roe* v. *Wade*. At the last moment, Mosby was persuaded to take a shorter drive on down to spend the weekend with our sister-in-law in southern Virginia. There Mosby regaled my brother's witty wife with tales of us three sisters sitting in an empty West Palm Beach movie theater wildly cheering *Thelma and Louise*. Except we didn't like the car-off-the-cliff suicide. "We'd have changed our 'margaritas-by-the-sea, mamacita,' Mexico plans and found another backroad," Mosby declared. "Maybe deep into the Badlands."

Much of what I first learned about wandering and being "bad enough to be yourself," as Aunt Mary Leola calls it, I learned from my aunts; most of what I learned about the lifelong journey of friendship I learned from my siblings. When we're all as old as Miss Eula and Miss Louise and in our own nursing home—perhaps we'll inherit it from Nettie Mae, Donna Ruth, and Mary Leola—our next generation will carry us, singing, as sisters take to the road.

# II

# THE ART OF THE SMALL

# THE SACREDNESS
# OF CHORES

*For C.H.*

One bright May morning, my arms piled high with clean, freshly folded laundry, I walked up to my housemate and dear friend's room and discovered that she'd taken her life. B.J. lay on that pale green carpet as if fallen from a great height, one hand outstretched. I did not see the gun gleaming like a dark fist at her temple as I knelt down to grab her wrist. Not dead, I thought, teeth chattering, just hurt. I had never seen anyone so hurt. Fumbling with her wrist, I finally felt a thready pulse against my forefinger—but it was only my own heart beating. I was so cold. Never have I felt that bone-deep shiver and chill. Her body was warm with sunlight, even though its own inner warmth was gone.

Then I saw her face, the eyelids darkly swollen, shut. From her nose and mouth ran congealed rushes of blood, a red so brilliant and dense that I remembered my sister saying that she'd once watched a heart explode on the operating table as she assisted a surgery, that it bloomed upward from the body like a rose bursting open. For a moment I jumped up, then fell right down, legs buckling. I again took B.J.'s hand, thinking somehow my touch might spare her the sight of herself.

But it was I who needed sparing. Alongside B.J.'s dead body, I knelt on all fours and howled until suddenly I heard a far-off accompaniment. It was a thud-thud, not of footsteps up the stairs but of something from deep within the bowels of the house itself. I listened, head cocked like an animal, listening with my eyes. And only after a time did I recognize the spin of the dryer. Then the thumping stopped and a piercing buzz began. It summoned me, this shrill signal, to stand upright, to leave the dead, to go downstairs and open the dryer door. More clean clothes tumbled into my arms, and I buried my face in the warm, fragrant cotton and colorful flannel. And because I could not carry B.J.'s body alone, because she no longer carried herself, I bunched her clean laundry against my chest and called for help. Then I carefully folded every sock and cotton camisole, every blouse and nightgown until the sirens stopped at my door.

It was so breathtakingly swift, so complete, B.J.'s leave-taking of her body, of her son and family and friends; and, though in my mind some part of me will always be howling on all fours in fury and grief over her brutal abandonment, there also lingers with me these six years later the exact weight and clean smell of her laundry.

After sharing domestic chores for six months, B.J. and I had struck a bargain: I did laundry and vacuumed; she did dishes and dusting. We shared scouring bathrooms, cooking, and the yard work, which was a kind of desultory dance between dandelions and an ancient push mower that mangled more than it trimmed. On the after-noon of B.J.'s death, I found myself sitting absolutely still in the kitchen. I stared at the bright haze of sunlight off Lake Washington, the silly burble of my coffee cheerful on the stove, the whir of the fridge, its rhythm loud and labored. I thought of the food inside this stupid, square, and noisy box—*Let it all rot and die!* At the same moment I remembered dully, *I should defrost that fridge.* It had been on my list of chores for the day, right after the laundry.

My morning list for that May day had read:

1) Finish Chapter 10
2) Laundry
3) Defrost fridge
4) Meet P.N. in the Market (check for rhubarb)

I gazed at the little list, and it seemed so earnest, so busy, so foolish. What did defrosting fridges, making a strawberry-rhubarb pie, or even finishing a chapter have to do with anything when all the while I'd scribbled that list my friend had been dead upstairs? The coroner said she'd died deep in the night while I lay down the hall sleeping, practicing for my own death.

I looked despairingly down at my clothes and realized I was still in my pajamas, the ones I'd bought in imitation of Lauren Bacall, the ones I'd rolled up at wrist and ankle, the ones, I realized now, must also be washed clean. It was only when I threw my pajamas in the washer, slathered Cheer on the load, and turned on the churn-ing machine that I found myself crying, kneeling on the cold cement floor and at last lamenting. It was safe enough to sob—the world had not stopped spinning, just as this washing machine spun and spun its little load through all its warm, delicate cycles.

This is how my friends found me. First, Paula, who arrived and busied herself during all the unexpected official paperwork of death by mowing the lawn furiously, up and down outside as if her precise patterns in the scraggly grass could bring order back to my little yard, my small world. Two days later, when I decided to leave this house, my friends Laura and Susan came heroically armed with buckets, Fantastik, and huge, brightly colored sponges to scrub and scour and spend hours on their hands and knees, a final cleansing of B.J.'s room, a kind of womanly worship. I put Alberta Hunter on the stereo, and we all got down on the floor, crying and cleaning. As we left the house for the last time, it shone in the sun, welcoming. Others would live here and wake up to the lapping lake, the coffee, fresh laundry. This house was again ready for life, life abundant.

Those mundane tasks that sunny May ten years ago have forever changed my sense of daily life. Those simple chores, both solitary and in the company of other women, were my first comfort in what was also my first death. The smell of Comet is forever linked with consolation, the spin of a dryer with survival, the syncopated chant of women scrubbing with the racial memory of reverence.

"Cleaning is incantation, physical prayer," says a friend who is an artist. "You create a small and ordered sacred place that has been touched a thousand times by your hands. It's a ritual of caring."

"The actual cleaning is sometimes secondary to the

mental housekeeping that takes place," adds my friend Rebecca, who has always made her living with her hands, either gardening or massaging. "Cleaning your house is like pruning a tree. The house and the tree are both alive. You take care of the debris first, then stand back to look at the true form—and that clarity, that original vision is what happens in the mind."

Stevie Smith, the British poet, commented that she dreamt up some of her best poems while "Hoovering." I have also opted for the vacuuming chores in my own household because the *rush* and *woosh* of the Kirby, its solid paths on the thick carpet tell me where I've been, where I am, and exactly where I want to go.

All of us claim territory. Traditionally the masculine way is to mark territory by scent, by song, by a boast, a show of power, a pile of weapons: "This is mine, do not enter or you'll reckon with me!" The feminine claiming is perhaps a fierce physical possessing of the space by adorning home with spells, magic, or brightly waving scarves in trees, as do the aborigines, who put powerful altars near their hearths both for worship and to summon protective guardian spirits.

In my current household, upon hearing that our rental home was to be scrutinized by potential buyers, my two housemates and I broke all real estate rules by staying home and doing our Saturday morning chores. While the house buyers perused, I maneuvered the noisiest vacuum this side of Seattle; one housemate ran the dishwasher and slung wet laundry everywhere, like so many volunteer scarecrow troops; my other housemate followed the harried home buyers from room to room wielding a defending dust mop. She actually sprayed the real estate agent with her lemon Pledge. Such was the territorial claiming of womanly warriors—and no prospective buyers have yet to make an offer these five months later.

Cleaning has long been women's work. For years women have borne the archetype of body, darkness, the erotic, the unclean, the Earth. This association has often imprisoned women in the home and trapped men in the world. Thus, leaving the home is traditionally associated with the heroic explorer, the powerful "man of the world," while the housework is seen as trivial, timid, uninspired, menial labor left to servants. But we are all in service to our homes, as well as our homeland of Earth.

For years environmentalists have been educating us to recognize that the whole wide world *is* our home; we cannot leave the world, or transcend it, or truly throw anything away. We must learn to be here. If women claim the world the way they already have their homes and if men claim their homes as fervently as they have the world, what might we create?

But instead of men and women creating their own homes, more and more people are leaving the home chores and ritual cleanings to hired hands. Are there some deep losses we all might incur from *not* cleaning up after ourselves? I suspect that doing our own chores is everyone's calling, no matter what our other important jobs. There is some sacredness in this daily, thoughtful, and very grounding housework that we cannot afford to lose if we are to be whole, integrated.

"Just getting down on my hands and knees and scouring the bathroom is like cleaning my soul," says a male friend. He adds with a laugh, "It shines—not necessarily my soul—but that white porcelain. And I feel new, like I've forgiven myself something."

Another of my men friends tells of his mother's death. When she, a meticulous cleaner, died, he stayed on alone in her house for three days and put everything right and tidy. "I felt very close to my mother then," he says. "After all, she had taught me how to clean."

Chores are a child's first work, though they are often presented in the form of play. Girls play house, and boys spend hours running toy trucks over miniature mud mountains. Before we even teach children to speak, we instruct them in their separate chores, and so we shape the world, the future. Somewhere along the line, society quit expecting boys to clean up their rooms, insisting they order the outside world instead. If I were a man, I would feel this as a loss, a wisdom and honor denied me and my home.

Among my friends, no matter their living situation, cleaning is a crucial issue. Perhaps it is simply the symbol of how we treat what we love. Some people clean like Lady Macbeth—"Out, damned spot!" Others clean haphazardly, or methodically, earnestly or devotedly. One of my housemates, Lynettie Sue, cleans as a way of understanding and organizing her life. From room to room she goes, sighing with satisfaction, as under her broom and dust rag and window-washing squeegee the world must give way to her scrutiny, her vision of a higher order suggested by perfectly folded sheets and a piano that looks spit shined. She is particularly imperious in the bathroom, being a microbiologist and knowing well that those telltale bits of black mold on the shower ceiling are unhealthy organisms. I teasingly beg her, "Don't take me to Comet-witz," when she suggests my upstairs bathroom looks like a biologist's field trip, "*not* cleaning concentration camp!" But I have found, under her diligence, a luxury that nothing except lounging in a hot, sparkling clean bathtub can give me.

Cleaning can be an art. I've often spent a Saturday morning dancing on the freeway of love right in the middle of my living room with Aretha and a vacuum. I admit to practicing arcane rites of exorcism as deep as psychoanalysis by simply cutting up ex-lovers' clothes to use as rags for those deep-down, won't-go-away cleaning jobs like stains on a rug, on a heart. Most recently cleaning came to my rescue when I received the final galley proofs for my novel in the mail with the dire red rubber stamp RETURN: 36-HOUR PROOF." What did I do with only three days to read and correct my entire book? I spent the first day and a half in a frenzy of old-fashioned, whirlwind spring cleaning that shook the spiders from the rafters and my soul. The book was a breeze after my walk-in winter closet.

When we clean up after ourselves, whether it's a spilled jar, a broken chair, a disorganized study, or a death, we can see and reflect upon our own life and perhaps envision a new way that won't be so broken, so violent, so unconscious. By cleaning up our own homes we take responsibility for ourselves and for preserving what we love. But if our attitude is "my kingdom is not of this world," then there is a disturbing possibility that we'll finally do away with the world rather than clean it or ourselves. The feminine attitude of getting down on our hands and knees to scour—and at the most primitive level look at what needs cleaning—deserves our attention. For in this gesture of bended knees is some humility, some meditation, some time to recognize the first foundation of our homes.

It was a simple washing machine and dryer that got me to my knees that day my friend died—in horror, in mourning, in surrender not to death but to survival. It was a homing instinct that grounded me and made me want to stay on. To this day I have a ritual of running the washer and dryer while I am in my study at work. There is no more comforting sound to me than the spinning of that washer or dryer. It is the whole world spinning in there, cleansing itself and me.

As long as the washer and dryer spin, I tell myself, I am safe and those I love may choose to keep living alongside me. For there is laundry to be done and so many chores—chores of the living. There is so much to be remembered under the dust of our old contempt for cleaning up after ourselves, picking up our own socks. There is much to be swept away and shined bright and scrubbed down to its deepest, most illuminating level. Think of all the chores we have yet to do, quietly and on our knees—because home is holy.

# LIFE IS A MUSICAL

*For R.W.*

When the day is too gray, when the typewriter is too loud, after a lovers' quarrel, when a sister calls with another family horror story, when the phone never stops and those unanswered messages blink on my machine like angry, red eyes—I tune out my life and turn up the music. Not my favorite public radio station but my own personal frequency—I have my own soul's station. It is somewhere on the dial between Mozart's *Magic Flute,* the gospel-stomping tiger growl of Miss Aretha Franklin, Motown's deep dance 'n' strut, and the singing story of Broadway musicals.

Whether it's Katie Webster's Swamp Boogie Queen singing "Try a Little Tenderness," or a South American samba, whether it's the Persuasions crooning "Let It Be" or that throbbing baritone solo "Other Pleasures" from *Aspects of Love,* my musical solace is so complete it surrounds me in a mellifluous bubble like a placenta of sound. To paraphrase the visionary Stevie Wonder, I have learned to survive by making sound tracks in my own particular key of life.

For years now I've made what I call "tapes against terror" to hide me away from the noisy yak and call of the outside world. These homemade productions are dubbed Mermaid Music; sometimes I send them to friends for birthdays and feel the pleasure of playing personal disc jockey to accompany their lives too. Among my siblings, we now exchange music tapes instead of letters. It is particularly gratifying to hear my nieces and nephews singing along to my tapes, as another generation inherits our family frequency.

I trace making my musical escapes to a childhood of moving around. As we packed the cardboard boxes with our every belonging—sometimes we hadn't even bothered to unpack our dresses from those convenient hanging garment containers provided by the last moving company—the singing began. From every corner of the emptying house, we'd hear the harmonies: my father a walking bass as he heaved-ho in the basement; my mother's soprano sometimes shrill and sharp as the breaking glass in the kitchen; my little brother between pure falsetto and a tenor so perfect we knew he'd stopped packing his room simply to sing; my sisters and I weaving between soprano and first and second alto from our bedrooms as we traded and swapped possessions for our next life. At last gathered in the clean, white space that was once our house, we'd hold hands and sing "Auld Lang Syne." Piling into the station wagon, with the cat in a wooden box with slats for air holes, Mother would shift into a rousing hymn, "We'll Leave It All Behind," or sometimes, if she was mutinously happy to hightail it out of some small "burg" as she called them, she'd lead us into "Shuffle Off to Buffalo," substituting wherever we were moving for the last word. "Chattanooga Choo Choo" and "California, Here We Come" were her standard favorites for leave-taking. If, as we drove past our schools and our friends' houses for the last time, the harmonies in the backseat faltered, Mother might remind us that choirs of angels never stayed long in one place singing because the whole world needed music. Father might suggest some slower songs, as long as they weren't sad.

In all the shifting landscapes and faces of my childhood, what stays the same is the music. First, there was my mother's music, which seems now to have entered effortlessly into her children's minds as if we were tiny tape recorders: the mild, sweetly suave Mills Brothers, Mitch Miller's upbeat swing, the close sibling harmonies of the Andrews Sisters, and always the church music, the heartfelt Sunday singing, which is the only thing I ever miss since leaving that tight fellowship of Southern Baptist believers.

Ever since I can remember—certainly I have flashes of being bounced around in the floating dark of my mother's womb as she tap-danced on the church organ pedals, sang at the top of her voice, and boogied across the keys—there has been this music. It is the only counterpoint to, the only salvation from a sermon that paralyzes the soul into submitting to a jealous God. From the beginning, music was an alternative to that hellfire terror. I can still hear it: a preacher's voice, first a boom, then a purr that raises into a hiss and howl to summon that holy hurricane of fire and brimstone. But after enduring the scourge of sins, there came the choir. Cooing and shushing, mercy at last fell upon those of us left on an Earth that this God had long ago abandoned. Listening to the full-bodied harmonies, I could close my eyes and heretically wonder, Wasn't Heaven still here?

*Yessss, hallelujah, still here ... Hush, can't you hear?* the choir murmured like so many mammies' lullabies. Then silence, as a small woman stepped forward, her rapt vibrato shimmering like humid heat lightning right before rain. Or a baritone dropping his woes and his dulcet voice low as a cello, caressing a whole congregation. If we were blessed that Sunday, there might be a shorter sermon and a "songfest" with harmonies we could hear in our heads, syncopating, counterpointing in a lovely braid of bright sound that beckoned us. *Sing now, brothers and sisters.* And we were many voices making one song. The fundamental fear was gone; weren't we already angels in Heaven?

Now that I am forty and have been what my family pityingly refers to as "settled-down" for ten years, now that I am so far backslid from the fellowship of the Southern Baptist believers, now that I no longer even make top ten on my mother's prayer list, now that the terror of Hell has been replaced by the terror of living, I still find myself calling upon my homemade choirs to accompany me in my car, to surround my study or kitchen and sing back the demons of daily life. Sometimes I've even caught myself slipping another tape against terror into the stereo and singing a distracted riff of my mother's favorite, "We'll Leave It All Behind."

During the recent holy war between the United States and Iraq, with the apocalyptic rhetoric about "Satan" and "infidels" eerily reminiscent of southern revivals—Mermaid Music was working long hours to meet my own and my friends' wartime demands. To offset NPR's daily interviews with military experts commenting on the allied video-war air strikes with the zealous aplomb of sportscasters, I'd surrender to the tender tenor of Aaron Neville singing "With God on Our Side" or "Will the Circle Be Unbroken?" As I drove along freeways where phosphorescent orange bumper stickers shouted USA KICKS BUTT! or OPERATION DESERT STORM, as if it were a souvenir banner of a hot vacation spot, I wondered that there was no music for the Gulf War. Where were the songs like "My Buddy" or "It's a Long Way to Tipperary"?

During the last days of the war, I relied upon Bach's Violin Concerto in D Minor, the fierce longing of Jacqueline DePres's cello, Fauré's Requiem and, as always, Mozart. On a particularly bad day, between the Pentagon press conferences—men with pointers, target maps, smart-bomb videos, and a doublespeak war doggerel that called bombing "servicing a target"—I made a beeline to my public library and checked out every musical from *Oklahoma* to *Miss Saigon*. I made a tape entitled "Life Is a Musical" and divided it into three sections: (1) Love Found in Strange Places, (2) Love Lost Everywhere, and (3) Love Returns. It was astonishing how songs from vastly different time periods and places segued together. My favorite storyline riff is "Empty Chairs at Empty Tables," from *Les Misérables* to "The American Dream" from *Miss Saigon* to "Carefully Taught" from *South Pacific* to "Don't Cry for Me, Argentina," from *Evita* to "Bring Him Home" from *Les Misérables*. When I sent copies out to a select group of musicals-loving friends, it was as if we were all together at a candlelight mass or cross-continent communion, trying to imagine a war where bombs fell.

Playing my own tapes against terror is a way to document and summon back the necessities that mothered them. For example, "My Funny Valentine," with its Billie Holiday/Sarah Vaughan/Ella Fitzgerald/Alberta Hunter blues and ebullience is still a favorite, long after that lover has gone. Upon hearing that an old friend had bone cancer, I made him a tape called "Music to Heal By," which included the Delta Rhythm Boys' version of "Dry Bones." My friend wrote to say it was the first time he'd laughed in a long time. Now he's making his own tapes. After a writer friend of mine drank herself to death, I felt so bereft—since, after all, we'd planned to retire to the Black Hole Nursing Home for Wayward Writers together—that I made a tape called "The Ten Commandments of Love, or Southern Baptists Beware!" It's every song I ever slow-danced to or memorized in the sweaty backseat of a borrowed car as my date and I broke Sunday school rules on Saturday night. Declared by my siblings and southern pals to have gone into "metal" (their word for platinum or gold), it includes Etta James's soaring "At Last," Sam Cooke's silky "Wonderful World," and a steamy duet of "634-5789" with Robert Cray and Tina Turner. It's a great tape for getting in the mood.

Since ancient times, the Chinese have believed that certain sounds can balance and heal. In acupressure, for example, each organ has a sound. Listening to a healthy heart, an astute healer can hear laughter or, if there is disease, wind. The gallbladder shouts; the stomach speaks in a singsong, sometimes overly sympathetic voice; and the kidney, ever the perfectionist, groans. Sighs can be a sign of liver ailments, and the pitch of a person's voice can tell a story of that body's health just as well as a tongue. In some Taoist practices to enhance longevity, re-creating the sounds of certain organs can strengthen and tone them. For example, the *whuuuh whuuuh* sound of the kidney can revitalize the adrenals, fortifying the immune system. If one cannot take time to sing in the key of every organ, I'd suggest Chinese wind chimes like the ones that grace my back porch. When a strong salt wind blows off the beach, my chimes, which are perfectly pitched to a five-element Chinese scale, play an impromptu arpeggio—a momentary transport to some monastic garden, a Shangri-la of sound. Scientific studies report that the actual sound of nature resonates at the level of eight hertz; by comparison, a refrigerator reverberates at eighty hertz. Is it any wonder some of us need to return to a musical womb to retreat from such technological onslaughts to our nervous systems?

In fact, our time in the womb is not at all quiet; it is a noisy symphony of voices, lower-tract rumbles, whirrings like waterfalls, and white noise. One of my friends found that if she played a tape of the roar of her sturdy Kirby vacuum cleaner, the sound immediately put her boisterous newborn twins to sleep. I have another friend whose entire house is wall-to-wall egg cartons, which absorb sound as well as enhance his audiophilic tendencies. I've visited houses that sound like living inside an aquarium, where pleasant underwater burbles from elaborate tropical fish tanks drown out the world. I've also entered homes where cuckoo clocks, grandfather chimes, and deep gongs count the hours so that I felt I was inside a ticking time bomb. Consciously or unconsciously we all make sound tracks to underscore our lives.

Mermaid Music has allowed me to enter a reverie of song, a backstage "smaller-than-life" sojourn away from all the stresses. Right now I'm at work on two dance tapes for a summer roll-up-the-rug party. Entitled "Bop till You Drop" and "Bad Girls," the tapes defy all hearers not to kick up their heels with such all-time hits as "Heat Wave" and "I Heard It Through the Grapevine," as well as the ever-popular "R-E-S-P-E-C-T." Of course, I've had requests for sequels and am at work on "Life Is a Musical II" divided into (1) "Falling," (2) "Feeling," and (3) "Forever Ruined/Recovery." It flows from "People Will Say We're in Love" to "Happy Talk" to "Just You Wait, Henry Higgins!"

My siblings say I should sell my tapes against terror on late-night TV in the company of such classics as Veg-O-Matics and "Elvis Lives" medleys. The idea fills me with horror. After all, there are copyright violations cops who come like revenuers in the dark of the night to bust local moonshiners and music makers. I'd rather stay strictly small-time and nonprofit, like that long-ago lullaby service I had in college, a trio of nannies against nightmares. But if anyone out there in music land is making his or her own tapes against terror, I'd be open to an exchange. After all, it's better than bombs through the mail or collecting baseball cards.

So tune in, and maybe we'll find ourselves on the same frequency. On this lifelong Freeway of Love, I just want to be an Earth Angel with my Magic Flute. Because after all, Everybody Plays the Fool and Ain't Nobody's Business If I Do.

# STUFF AS DREAMS
# ARE MADE ON

The first time I believed that dream life might be as important as daily life was the year we lived across the street from the Atlantic Ocean and a dream saved my brother's life. I was seven and shared a bedroom with my baby brother. At night, radiators steaming, ocean waves as intimate and steady as our own breathing, I'd lie in my little bed, one arm stretched out through the wooden bars of my brother's crib. In rhythm to a lullaby my grandfather had inherited from his mammy and passed along to me, I'd sing and pat my brother's small back like a miniature island across which soon both our dreams would stretch out and into some vast ocean of sleep.

> Sail, baby, sail
> Out across the sea
> Only don't forget to sail
> Back again to me

I'd sing, pat that sweetly powdered back, and we'd both tack off into the night wind.

But one night my brother drifted too far. Of course, I was far away, too. I was in a dream that took much of its realistic detail from the Revere Beach amusement park we passed every day on our way to school in that run-down suburb of Boston. In the dream was the same cockamamie roller coaster, the submarine sandwich stand where we always squandered our allowances, and the Big Tent.

The Big Tent was really big; in fact, it looked like an amphitheater. And I was even smaller than a child. I was more the size of my infant brother. In my dream I flew straight into this Big Tent, not bothering with a ticket; even in a dream it seemed this was the wrong thing to do. A carnival barker called, "Everyone with tickets can leave," and the crowd stampeded out. I soon saw why: A giant fat lady, kind of like a King Kong in pink tights and red polka-dot panties, crashed into the Big Tent, making right for me. I gazed up and saw the ceiling was now a wide, polka-dot whiteness descending, and I screamed until I couldn't breathe. Down, down came the bottom, and then I was snuffed out, suffocated by spacious, spotted silk.

My screams summoned my father, who was immediately beside my bed. But then he started screaming, too. He threw my robe toward me; it thwacked the air, its plaid wool wrapping around my head, mummylike. I couldn't hear what Father was yelling—something about ice and the baby basin we used to give my brother baths. Barefooted, I ran for the ice and basin, returning to find my father holding my brother aloft. The baby was blue, naked, stretched flat and rigid; he was no longer a body but a board with familiar bumps.

Father laid my brother in the basin and packed him in three trays of ice. To this day I cannot hear the sound of champagne bottles in a bucket without wincing, because that was the sound of my brother's body convulsing under ice.

"Make your hand into a lobster claw," my father ordered, and then he used my fingers like pincers to pull my brother's tongue out, holding it tightly. It felt like the time I'd unshelled a snail and been horrified to see that wobbly creature so very vulnerable without his hard, outer sheath; it hurt me to look at it for long.

But I could not help looking at my brother's body. He jerked with so much power I knew then that we must be more than a physical presence. For what moved through him, and by connection us, could only be called a great current. The only thing I'd ever felt as powerful as my baby brother's energy was a West Coast undertow that once took me until I breathed water. I had not died in the Pacific Ocean undertow, nor did my brother from his sudden high fever's convulsion.

But the doctor said he would have died within minutes had it not been for my nightmare that woke Father.

"What did you dream, anyway?" the doctor asked as he lay a supple, still sleeping baby back in the crib. My brother was no longer blue; he even cooed in his sleep like a mourning dove.

"I dreamed the fat lady sat down on me," I said.

"You were suffocating, then?" the doctor asked in a calm voice. "Well, so was your brother." Then he explained about babies and swallowing tongues.

I didn't like all the details. I tuned the doctor out and went back to sleep, only to find the Big Tent waiting for me. But this time I climbed up a chair as high as a mountain. As the fat lady moved to sit down on me again, I yelled up to her. She noticed me as she might a gnat, but she didn't sit down. Instead she leaned over, and her face, as big as a planet, loomed. Then she was laughing, crossing her tree-trunk arms as she waited for me to explain myself. I wasn't afraid anymore, but I also didn't know how to talk to the fat lady with her way up there and me way down on my wooden plateau. So we both simply waited, one for the other.

For years the Big Tent and fat lady waited for me. Every October around the date of my brother's long-ago fever, I used to have the same nightmare.

From the age of seven and that life-saving dream, I've developed the habit of asking myself questions before I go to bed at night, hoping my dreams might answer. Once I asked a dreamy question about a potential lover and was told by a brusque dream friend, who vaguely resembled my biology teacher, Mrs. Chopsky, that I needed new socks because mine were so thick my feet didn't touch ground. Of course, Mrs. Chopsky was right—love, or the longing for it, had ungrounded me so that my dreams had to step right in and be more realistic.

Recently after many years' absence, the fat lady visited me again in my dreams. This time she was out of costume, out of the Big Tent. In fact, she was no longer the cartoon that my fear had first made of her. She was fully present, and, even though I was still smaller, I met her. I cannot say yet that I am comfortable with her, even in my dreams. I tell myself often that I am too small for the big picture, perhaps the Big Tent. But she will wait for me as she always has.

She waits for me the way I am learning to wait for myself before I take those conscious plunges into my unconscious depths, my own dreams. She waits for me much the way that the Atlantic Ocean waited all during long New England winters for us children to again enter her commanding waves, mindful of the undertow.

And when I think of dreaming, I believe that my dreams live alongside my daily life the way that ocean moved right across the busy street from our apartment house. We lived as children on the edge of infinity; we live as adults on the edge of our dreams. Perhaps we don't need any other vessel to go where we need to go. With sleep as our ship, we can sail, we can sail.

# THE ALL-HOURS LULLABY
# SERVICE

*For Laurel Anne and D.G.*

When I was in school, back in the Berkeley of 1968, there were so many reasons we couldn't sleep. There were sit-ins and love-ins, there were all-night study and primal scream sessions, there was the joy of sex and the angst of the Vietnam War, there were dream workshops and astral traveling—there was, in fact, everything that could be done politically, psychologically, and sexually lying down, except something very simple and vital: sleep.

Of course, at the University of California (at the Davis campus, where I fled after one of my friends was hospitalized, having been teargassed in the Berkeley library during Reagan's response to People's Park), there was an experimental program for freshmen. Called Self and Society, the program offered university credits for living and participating in a psychological study that we later realized was a hybrid of Esalen and the Harrad experiment.

It was a difficult first year, with several suicides, many busts in this drug haven of a dormitory, and too many close encounters of the unkind, the untrained, the unknown. It, the unknown, stretched out, even for us jaded eighteen-year-olds, into brief futures. No one expected to live much past thirty; nuclear war or our own burnout would spare us the decrepitude, if not wisdom, of old age. But I think more difficult for us than contemplating the end of the world, the war, was discovering that we were, after all, still very young and somehow still virgin. We knew so much about empathy, so little about intimacy. And we deflowered flower children, for all our political savvy, were strangers to the slow and sweet romance of self-restraint.

So it was no wonder we couldn't sleep alone; and even after sex, we couldn't sleep together. Who could rest when the world was such a wreck? We could feel it turning, spinning, veering off course right under our beds— the big, broken world was our boogeyman.

One night one of us in Self and Society was brave or innocent enough to look under his bed and meet that boogeyman. Antonio was a small fellow from a vast Italian family; before college he'd longed to be a priest. Now he was a pusher, and he was also crouched in the duck-and-cover position in the middle of his dorm room, catatonic; the needle on his stereo had stuck, playing over and over, "I am a rock, I am an iiiiiii...."

My two friends and I were in the stairwell singing. We were very serious singers, having discovered that in all the swirl of this psychological experiment, we guinea pigs could raise our voices, not in protest or praise but in three-part harmony. We were distracted from our syncopated parts by Simon and Garfunkel astutter next door. All we heard was "aiiieee ... aieeeee," which I've since learned are the syllables of lament in Greek. Aggrieved, we entered Antonio's room and found him a zombie.

His roommate was gone; she might have provided some clue to his condition. In our dorm, boys and girls lived in the same rooms, shared the same bathrooms, practiced the art of eyelining and shaving before the same mirrors. So there was an abnormally low incidence of mating in Self and Society. We went outside for passion; anything else was incest. But Antonio's roommate was an exception. Had she just walked out on her would-be priest and now bunkmate? No, said someone wandering by stoned in the hallway. She'd gone to the health center with her encounter-group leader to get help. Meanwhile, there was nothing to do but wait.

It was odd that there was no ambulance, no one to take Antonio away, for surely he was in some extremity of pain or injury; we just couldn't see the wound. I don't exactly remember how it happened, whether we were bored—catatonics really don't capture the imagination after the initial shock—or being sympathetic, but we began to sing. Soon we were soaring. Our three parts for once sounded perfect even without the resonance of the stairwell. We slid into our beloved songs, the free range of our voices like sailing together on the same boat. And we made our own wind.

During my grandfather's favorite lullaby, Antonio, though still gone, began to breathe in exact rhythm with us. It was like having a fourth part to the harmony. We included him like a very small child whose body isn't bellows or verbal enough to sing but is right alongside us.

The lullaby went on forever. We were afraid if we stopped singing Antonio might go away again, even stop breathing, drown, man overboard.

As our lullaby finally faded, Antonio slowly hunched his back, stretched his arms out before him as if in some yoga posture, and then glanced up at us, bewildered. "Sorry," he said, still not quite all in residence, "I guess I got stuck."

"So was your record," was all we could think to say before his roommate returned with the nurse from the health center.

"Overdose?" asked the nurse with a certain weariness. "Astral traveling? Bad trip?"

"I think he just needed to sleep," said Antonio's girl-friend softly. "We haven't had much lately." She looked so tired, the dark and deep skin beneath her eyes like bruises.

"Please come back," Antonio told us as the nurse took him away. "Come back and sing to me."

Antonio did not come back to Self and Society. We never heard what happened to him. Perhaps he is a priest somewhere, or a rock, or an island. But we kept singing that year. Word got out that we would come sing lullabies to those on bad trips. Soon we were getting calls almost every night. Eight floors of freaked-out freshmen kept us so busy that we actually started charging ten dollars a singing session. We got tagged the All-Hours and Insomniacs' Lullaby Service. We sang to bulimics to keep them from throwing up; we sang to anorexics while they forced food; we sang to students whom Quaaludes kept awake; we sang to those recovering from the latest encounter sessions; and we sang to all our peers who had been touched, felt, politicized, feminized, militarized—everything but harmonized.

Lullabies have a way of washing over the body and soul like a loving mammy's hand giving a bath, except on the inside. And for the singers it is also a comfort. Singing alongside someone who knows where your voice will go by the arch of an eyebrow, the slight crease of concentration in the lips, this being known and being present together without talk, without touch, with only the ebb and flow of harmony like Möbius strips of sound eternally moving in and out of the body with the breath—it is how I finally began to learn about intimacy.

My partners in that long-ago lullaby service still call cross-country; we don't talk much. We sing on the phone and send tapes back and forth. As my friends' voices play on the cassette, I again hear the harmonies come in my head like insights, like memories, and like all the years ahead now that we've survived into our forties. I have even begun to consider that it is perhaps a good time to bring back the All-Hours and Insomniacs' Lullaby Service.

Today we sing lullabies to our babies, but rarely to ourselves or one another. But I think perhaps now we veterans of the sixties might truly begin to sing lullabies together for all those years we sang protest songs and were so afraid of the world, of the boogeyman. They say children grow in their sleep. Perhaps now as grown-ups we need someone to sing us lullabies because even though we are adults, we haven't stopped growing. But like Antonio's wound, or like lullabies, all that grows in us is now on the inside and often in the dark.

# BATHING WITH
# MADAME BOVARY

*For L.B.*

I n dark Alaska winters," a fisherman friend told me, "if a man wants a woman's company, his cabin better have running water."

"Why?" I teased. "Don't you think women can rough it like men?"

"Sure they can." He grinned. "But women want hot baths in between. If you want to keep a woman in winter, water's the way."

I wondered at what my friend said—do baths belong more to the feminine than to the masculine? On an impromptu survey of my female friends, thirteen out of fifteen preferred baths to showers; of the same number of men asked, fourteen out of fifteen chose brisk showers over what one uncomfortable man called "stewing in my own juices."

As I write this now, I am in the tub. My skin is wonderfully wrinkled like stewed prunes, and the juices that steep my body are luxurious lavender, eucalyptus, melissa balm, and an East Indian bubble elixir called Treasures of the Sea—these fragrant beads turn the hot water a tranquil blue. I imagine I'm in my own Caribbean cove with all I need surrounding me: glacial Bourassa bottled water to drink, Mozart on the headphones, a candle glowing inside delicate wax colored like stained-glass windows. Across the blue tub balances a pine board, on which I have my writing pad, books, and loofah sponges. My feet now long for loofah and the rich cocoa butter massage that will soon coat and perfume these scoured feet as if I've just stepped from a vat of warm chocolate.

Every so often while writing, I sink beneath the tub desk and rest against my bath pillow shaped like a soft seashell to cushion my shoulders and sore neck. The triangle of trapezius muscles are a writer's bane; they seem always in spasm. But watery heat tenderly eases those knots and lets the muscles melt until they float the heavy head like so much seaweed flotsam adrift on a warm sea.

It is not the womb I'm after here; it is Neptunian nepenthe. I want to forget myself, loose the tense bonds and laws of gravity. The world flows and pulses with the feminine pull of Moon and ocean. Perhaps if our planet were a desert, our species might clean our skin with white sand. But as much as we Earth dwellers forget it, as single-minded as we were to name our entire planet for the only element we humans live upon—by rights this world should be named Sea, and maybe the whales call it that in their long, low lullabies—this planet orbiting the Sun looks so blue from outer space because seven-tenths of it belongs to water.

Why not then worship in the bath?

"What do you *do* in there for all that time?" an old boyfriend once asked me. There was a hint of fear in his voice, and fascination. "It's erotic, right?"

"What would you do if someone assigned you to take a bath for two hours?" I teased.

"Well ..." He brightened. "Maybe I'd make love to myself—that's the polite way of saying it."

"Then what?"

"I'd wash and scrub ..." He fell silent.

"Would you massage with expensive oils? Would you read Victorian novels or chat on the portable phone? Would you meditate or burn candles all round so that you floated in warmth and light like those bioluminescent creatures at the very bottom of the ocean who give off their own bright phosphorus as a by-product?"

"Stop!" he cried, both alarmed and lulled. "It's siren stuff. Your baths might as well be shipwreck for a man. We drown in mermaids' arms."

So I asked him into the bath. He chose sandalwood soap and almond milk bubbles. As we lay in the tub together, I scoured his feet with pumice stone, then rubbed his back with strong sponges. Tenderly we washed each other's hair with chamomile shampoo and lemongrass conditioner. As we sipped sparkling cider from plastic wineglasses, he lay back and sighed, eyes closed. I had never seen him more relaxed or vulnerable. That bath was the only time he ever told me he was in love with me. Shortly afterward we broke up.

"It was that bath," he said, to explain why he was going back to his ex-wife. "We should have waited until we knew one another better before we did ... *that.*"

We'd been lovers half a year before this bath. But he was right. We weren't ready. It was more intimate than lovemaking.

It is ironic that in our twentieth-century love, nineteenth-century eroticism seems improper at best—at worst a direct threat. Flaubert knew about deep intimacies of the bath. In *Madame Bovary* Emma is pursued by an adoring Rodolphe, who declares, "Oh, I think of you constantly.... One cannot fight fate! Or resist when the angels sing!" The effect of Rodolphe's passionate words upon Madame is telling. "Emma had never been told such things before and her pride stretched out luxuriously in the warmth of his words, as though she were relaxing in a hot bath."

To the nineteenth-century reader, the sinking of Madame Bovary into bath instead of bed was synonymous with intimacy. Still today, European men seem to take more baths than their American counterparts. An editor friend often came across her Italian boyfriend sunk deep in his elaborate, claw-footed tub, mineral salts instead of bubbles. Sometimes he did business in the bath with Dictaphone and calculator. Another friend lived many years with a Frenchman whose passion was to disappear into the bath, turn off the lights, and listen full-blast to the Grateful Dead. A Cuban man I know takes afternoon baths like daily siestas.

I suspect one reason why most American men prefer showers is that they accept the Puritan equation between water and body. Showers are for baptism, cleaning, and cooling down unruly, too passionate flesh. One cleans one's body, lingering as little as possible on the sensual temptations of skin, curve, and private places. In contrast, Vergie, my stepgrandmother, used to bathe us grandchildren on her farm in a large tin washtub. She'd heat the well water on her wood stove and pour it over our heads and bodies; then she'd take a soft flannel cloth, suds it into a lather of Ivory, and proceed to "put y'all back together." Ever since she heard somewhere that the word *re-member* means to put back together a dismembered body, she saw her baths as a way of helping her grandchildren remember their bodies.

We learned the facts of life as we learned the lay of the land. Vergie taught us to take care of our bodies as she did her land. "Nothing sorrier than an old used-up person or field."

"Another thing." Vergie always finished her baths with a welcome cold rinse like a garden hose-down in midsummer. "No one owns your body but you. Just like nobody really owns the land."

If no one owns my body but me, who better to nurture and care for it than myself? If my body is my true home, why would I ever forsake or ravage it? Vergie is still very much alive. I believe her survival into active old age has much to do with tending her bountiful garden and taking good care of her own and others' bodies. For years she was a beautician, tending women's hair as if it were the most delicate, flowering vines. Because Vergie initiated me into the healing mysteries of bathing and "beautification," as she called her practice, I can look forward to a lifetime of ritual baths by way of remembering Vergie's wisdom, as well as my own body's.

Bathing our children and grandchildren is a mothering gift; bathing lovers is a sacrament of sensual love. But I believe the best that baths can give us is the simple yet rare act of self-knowledge. *Know thyself*—this includes knowing bodies. Bathing calls forth a self-scrutiny. Certainly an hour afloat with one's own imperfect thighs, belly, and derriere, a bath familiar with one's own cellulite and flaccid fault lines, is an exercise in self-acceptance. It is hard to transcend the body in a hot bath. One sinks into one's own physical and metaphysical depths. Who knows what lurks down there? Who knows what we might plumb about ourselves? Will our compassion for what we discover about ourselves be equaled by our tendency toward self-contempt?

I keep two pictures in my bathroom: One is a painting of a naked woman swimming with dolphins; the other is a 1972 framed silver print by the famous *Life* photojournalist W. Eugene Smith. Called "Tomoko in Her Bath," the darkly lit black-and-white photo shows a young Japanese girl, victim of mercury poisoning from a nearby chemical factory, which caused birth defects in many of her village's children. Tomoko's truncated, shriveled body, her twisted hands like flippers useless and afloat beside her body are almost unbearable to look at for long. What makes staring at the photograph possible is the rapt, unflinching compassion of the woman who floats Tomoko in her wide arms, all the while gazing gently down upon the child in all her deformity. This woman's arms and eyes take in everything—from misshapen hands to withered legs to a head thrown back in numb, physical despair.

In my mind, this is an image of the divine Mother bathing her broken child. This Mother does not judge human deformity or condemn it to eternal punishment. This Mother's mercy is a clear-eyed witness to what cripples us. I have gazed deeply at this photo while lying in my own bath, whenever the deforming demons of my inner critic weigh heavily on me, body and soul. I have apprenticed myself to learning this kind feminine compassion, which embraces perhaps especially what is most hideous and dark about me. This is true baptism to me. If God the Father's forgiveness of this world comes at the cost of sacrificing His Son, it is God the Mother who takes that body down from the cross and bathes its broken bones and fatal wounds.

The photographer of "Tomoko in Her Bath" was critically wounded as a war correspondent during the 1945 invasion of Okinawa. During his painful convalescence, he endured thirty-two operations. He well understood physical suffering and compassion. His heart-stirring photo essay "Minamata" (1975) exposed the chemical company's mercury poisoning of Japanese children to a horrified world. For his revelations, Smith was harassed, driven out of the village, and severely beaten. Many people believe that he never recovered from these beatings and that they led directly to his death in 1978. It is a sad irony that the compassion of a clear-eyed witness can be so dangerous.

Compassion for one's self and others is not a blissful denial nor is it an easy embrace of darkness. Seeing one's self clearly and witnessing others in all their wide range of being is often harrowing. And that is why in my bathroom there is that double vision to help me in my bath— the playfulness of the dolphins as well as the dive into my own darkness.

Perhaps this descent is what made one of the men in my survey uncomfortable; perhaps this is the "stewing" in one's own self that he so feared. Even Madame Bovary had to reckon with it and, so, herself. As Rodolphe, "certain of her love," retreated, he "began to be careless." Emma grieved: "Gone were those tender words that had moved her to tears, those tempestuous embraces that had sent her frantic, the grand passion into which she had plunged seemed to be dwindling around her like a river sinking into its bed; she saw the slime at the bottom." The water imagery is apt. While water cleanses, it can also be troubled, polluted, full of "slime." Madame Bovary has bathed in Rodolphe's love; she will also sink into it and ultimately not survive her descent.

These days while bathing I like to imagine a modern ending for *Madame Bovary*. Instead of killing herself for love lost, she decides to take to her bath. There she spends days comforting herself with Damask Rose and Devon Violet bath seeds. Adrift in the steaming flower fragrance, Madame Bovary opens her eyes and sees her own body so recently abandoned, so longing for her lost lover's touch. She takes a sponge, sudsed with sandalwood, and strokes her long arms, her delicate legs, her floating breasts. Emma sighs and slips deeper into the bath, luminous with bubbles. She notices that her own skin gleams, too.

Only now can she look deeper into the slime also growing at the bottom of her own life—the financial ruin, the emotional debts her passions have run up as high as her fevers. She is bankrupt, body and soul. Should she simply sigh and drown herself in this bath? Should she really gulp arsenic stolen from her local chemist? Softly Emma hears a deep and familiar feminine voice, as if the water herself were speaking, soothing, cleansing. Emma closes her eyes and imagines there are mothering arms rocking her, a dark and compassionate face gazing down upon her as she weeps into the warm water. Can she, like her lovers, truly abandon this broken body? Slowly Emma eases herself from the bath as if she is newborn, as if she has at last remembered herself.

# THE EVIDENCE OF
# THINGS SEEN

What I witnessed one very early Christmas morning when I was seven has spoiled me for the rest of my life. Or, at least if not spoiled, then certainly it has made me more a stranger in the strange land of modern love.

That year my family made one of its many migrations—at Christmas we take airplanes and cross-country trips the way other people take Valium—to southern Missouri and the almost mythical small town of my grandparents. I say mythical because for my family, who never lived any longer than two years in the same place, my grandparents' small town held the dignity of Real Life because it continued with a regular and trustworthy ordinariness. We didn't see Grandmother and Grandfather flying off the face of the Earth every other year or so and landing in strange cities looking like little aliens who talked funny, laughed in all the wrong places, and wore anklets and noisy pink snow pants when all the other girls were wearing subtle woolens.

We had landed in Boston that year, my father on fellowship at Harvard; he lived among the library shelves and Mother traipsed around Boston looking in vain for a Southern Baptist church where the people didn't sing hymns slow with Yankee accents. For Christmas it was decided that we would travel to her home and find solace there for enduring a new year back in New England.

There are some years of our childhood that we remember in exact detail as if everything happens in some darkroom of the mind, each event developed indelibly. Memories of those particular years are like flash cards we learn from. What I saw that Christmas morning in my grandparents' small town is such a flash card—it was my first lesson in lovemaking.

In my grandparents' spacious gray house, the big people slept on the ground floor and we children braved the second story—"closer to God," Grandmother would say as she tucked us in, but we were not at all convinced. For one thing there was the attic door right smack dab in the bathroom and the obviously haunted North Room, where I, the oldest, had to sleep alone, as well as the South Room, which was all too intimate with the weeping willow that rasped against the roof. In between, and in the middle of the night, was that attic where I'd once seen a Yankee hiding, though my uncle swore it was just his old army outfit. We smelled trunks of rotting, before-our-time things in that attic and little creatures died there, as we could attest when Grandmother every so often swept and we saw stiff mice whisked away without funerals.

That Christmas we were quite concerned for Santa, who would have to enter our grandparents' house at its most dangerous peak—the attic. But we were not so afraid for Santa's safety that we would leave the attic door open in case he needed us to rescue him from that dread, dark place.

Besides, I was suspicious of Santa. I kept these heresies to myself and only discussed them with my classmate Peter. He was from Germany, an alien like myself, and I was assigned to teach him English after school. But what we really did was go to the beach and lie under a rowboat and play Sleeping Beauty. First he was the prince and woke me with a kiss, then I took my turn being that swashbuckling smoocher. Peter learned little English, but I learned a lot about what it felt like to have a warm, lithe body against mine, slow-dancing in the sand with the complete innocence of curiosity. Because he was from Europe, and had been schooled by a French governess, Mlle. Véronique, I believed Peter knew more about the world. When he told me that Santa was to adults what Sleeping Beauty and the Prince were to us—a pretend and playful presence—I took it on faith. What was more amazing and difficult to take on faith was Mlle. Véronique's suggestion that when big people made love they somehow entered one another's bodies in much the same mysterious and gift-giving way that Santa entered houses.

I could say that Christmas dawn when I stole downstairs from my haunted room to sit quietly on the cedar chest at the end of my grandparents' bed that I was really waiting for Santa to not appear. But what I was really waiting for was to watch what happened when big people made love.

My grandparents slept side-by-side in their big four-poster and the in-between, winter light over their white comforter made them look like those museum exhibits of woolly mammoths under the snow. Their faces as they slept were very pale, mouths open like baby birds, and I remember thinking how very young they looked in sleep, how expectant. I was expectant, too, and as the first sun slanted across their bed my grandfather gave a great kick just like a frog. Off went the covers! I fell back, horrified. I thought of Peter growing up into a Frog Prince and never turning back into the pretty little boy I loved to kiss. Maybe lovemaking changed people physically and they could not return to their right shape or form. I almost ran out of the room.

My grandparents lay near one another, their night-shirts wrapped around their spindly legs. Not touching, they slept soundly on their backs. I crept closer and saw that they breathed in perfect rhythm, their bellies rising and falling as if one breath moved through both their bodies. Then I, too, breathed deeply, now not at all afraid. I felt that somehow I was part of them—not between them or down at the end of the bed like the onlooker I had felt so much of my life. No, I felt *with* them as if that bed were one big body and we all fit just fine.

In my chest something moved and I felt more space inside my rib cage—a wide expanse that opened me from the inside out, not the way I'd seen adults crack open lob-sters but the way I'd watched big people open their mouths slowly when they were touched and then bow their heads and say, for once, absolutely nothing.

At that moment my grandmother opened her mouth and tilted her head slightly upward as if to receive, and then she did something so right for her I knew this was Grandmother's way of making love. She cooed, a low, throbbing sound in her throat like the way she spoke to birds when feeding them old bread. My grandfather's head tilted back too, and he answered her with a warbling, sweet snore.

Mesmerized, I watched as two hands softly moved out in perfect sync to clasp across that wide bed—clasp and capture one another and hold still as if this were not sleep but constancy. This was how big people made love, made me.

This, I would later whisper to Peter when I woke him from his dream with a kiss, this was lovemaking: two hands finding one another at exactly the right time, even while sleeping. This I could believe in, the way I'd witnessed my grandparents' bodies believe in one another without seeing, by simply reaching out in the dark.

What I told my sisters and brother that morning when I climbed the stairs was that Santa had come, though I, too, had passed through it in a dream. Because that morning when my grandparents awoke, they called me into their big bed and we three lay listening for Santa— who would always come to me, girlie, my grandfather said, even if I never saw him.

# HEARTBREAK HOTEL

Over the years, in rhythm to the ebb and flow of my romances, I've found myself checking in and out of a shelter I've come to call Heartbreak Hotel. Sometimes I go there in my mind, sometimes Heartbreak Hotel shares my actual street address; what is the same is what goes on here: a rest, a rite of passage, a healing, and finally a way of loving the world more truly because exiled from it.

In certain tribes when the heart suffers some death or loss, the women seclude themselves in the spiritual commune of the moon lodges while the men launch off into a long journey, perhaps a hunt or a vision quest. But in our peculiarly impatient and restless American way of intimacy, love on the lam, there is little time to practice this ritual of grief. Mourning is embarrassing, it is certainly antisocial, and sometimes it just seems downright rude.

And yet in Heartbreak Hotel I've discovered the welcome mat is always out for the weary, huddled masses of modern lovers who must seek shelter like so many home-less hearts. If in the old days there was the Foreign Legion for wounded-in-action soldiers and endless Edith Wharton ocean crossings for heroines with heart mur-murs, today we need nearby getaways. That's why Heart-break Hotels are never hard to find. They are just off the side streets of the great thoroughfares of romantic com-merce. In fact, I've noticed them nowadays popping up like prefabs on the erotic market, even more insistently than the condo of the couple.

Heartbreak Hotels are quite distinct pieces of prop-erty, depending upon the dominant sexual character of the heartbroken or the relationship itself. The hotels are no longer segregated, for a woman might well need to check herself in at an unself-consciously seedy masculine Heartbreak Hotel at least for a belt of bourbon and milk; just as a man might be comforted to be ensconced in the cozy breakfast nook of the feminine Heartbreak Hotel where a mammy who is also a wet nurse serves hot choco-late spiked with peppermint schnapps.

In the masculine Heartbreak Hotel the tenants never shave faces or legs; in the feminine Heartbreak Hotel, the lodgers eat popcorn and Snickers bars for supper. There is never sex; even flirtations make us flinch. In the feminine Heartbreak Hotel there are junk food deliveries made by stunning, but discreet and sympathetic, delivery people, all hours, all ears. One can order compassion with extra catsup or try a little tenderness with tartar sauce. But the delivery people, like the fast food they serve, have a schedule. They don't linger like any kind of real nourishment.

These delicious delivery people never go near the masculine Heartbreak Hotel. That's because in the masculine Heartbreak Hotel one doesn't eat, one drinks. There in the single residences of this transient hotel, the heartbroken don't have stomachs. They have guts. This masculine Heartbreak Hotel looks out on the wrong side of town. A railroad or subway track shudders nearby; neon glares, unblinking. Beneath a naked bulb is a slim, steel bed, a tacky bedstand where Gideon's Bible has been hocked for Wild Turkey, Camel unfiltereds, a deck of cards, a pair of fingernail clippers. Clip, clip, drip, drip of the broken sink. One reads only the graffiti scrawled on the wall. Perhaps there is a *Playboy* or *Cosmopolitan* rolled up like a blunt weapon, repeatedly rapped against the thigh in rhythm to some hangover hum in the head. Occasionally there is the sound of the magazine striking a glancing blow to the wall. This is *not* a call for help, nor is it a statement. It is a reflex of the heart in solitary confinement—or perhaps on death row—awaiting not a pardon but the final zap, the poison, the noose. *Let it come,* says the single resident in this masculine Heartbreak Hotel, *I dare you to take me any further down than I can take myself.*

If the masculine Heartbreak Hotel is an inner battleground, the feminine Heartbreak Hotel is like a camp pitched near enough to see the smoke and hear the wails of the dying, the deserted, the damned. As in all camps, there is a coziness even in this most primitive of conditions, the death of the heart. Of course, there is a front porch with rockers stretching the length. There is the night music of crickets or waves of mountain wind—anything that sighs in sync with us. Rooms are comfy, familiar, often rearranged to fit moods, whims, or whirlwind, heartfelt tidy attacks. Favorite foods are baked potatoes, banana cream pie, pasta with gluttonous amounts of pesto and glorious garlic. Oreos are stashed in convenient crevices, as are sweet Sherman's cigarettes, sherry, and delicate, finger-sized Almond Joys. There is a small refrigerator in the large bathroom with a garret ceiling. It offers driest Chablis, champagne splits, and Diet Pepsi. There is a telephone, a bookshelf with Victorian novels— *Wuthering Heights* a favorite wallow—and a twenty-pound box of Mr. Bubble. Down the hall waft strains of Patsy Cline's "I Fall to Pieces" or Joni Mitchell's "Oh, I could drink a case of you, darling, and I would still be on my feet...." Evenings in the feminine Heartbreak Hotel there are readings of old love letters, followed by well-meaning but sparsely attended workshops called "Intimacy in the 90s" or "Forgiveness 1A." Most lodgers wander off down memory lane, or onto the wide embrace of the front porch, up to the madwoman's attic, or into the softly lit, free massage and dream therapy rooms.

For all its luxurious mournfulness, the feminine Heartbreak Hotel is as difficult a stay as its masculine counterpart. To be so bereft while coddled by the familiar litter of one's love; to be alone yet surrounded by soulmates; to be in the dark during broad daylight—this is as dangerous a descent as the more daredevil masculine grief, the fighter jock who plays chicken with the Earth. For in the feminine Heartbreak Hotel, we are just as lost, no matter the trail we might leave of brightly colored M&M's or tea cozies.

It is in this willing wallow that the masculine and feminine Heartbreak Hotels meet. Yet there is a final, telling difference: length of stay. In the masculine Heartbreak Hotel, there are weekend, even hourly rates. As my friend Greg says flatly, "No guy would ever max out his MasterCard at Heartbreak Hotel." But in the feminine Heartbreak Hotel, lodgers sometimes linger for life. This contrast is also one of the only drawbacks to Heartbreak Hotel. Masculine mourners tend to grieve on the run or in singles' bars, sometimes carrying their unburdened sorrow right into the next relationship. This leads to cynicism; a fist can clench and unclench quickly—not so the heart. Then there are the feminine lodgers who survive on maintenance sorrow, dolefully expecting lovers to follow rules made for delivery people. It would be sadder still if only men checked into the masculine Heartbreak Hotel and women into the feminine. This exclusivity only encourages the segregation and solipsism that sends us to Heartbreak Hotel in the first place.

The feminine Heartbreak Hotel can borrow from the masculine their larger-than-life battle that becomes a true rite of passage; from this our hearts learn courage and the resilience of a working muscle. The masculine Heartbreak Hotel can integrate from the feminine the *being-with* one's own abiding pain, taking a rest from the front, from the warrior way, so that the heart might again embrace without fear, without expecting an enemy.

Whether we check into the masculine or feminine Heartbreak Hotels, whether we rent by the hour, the day, the year, and whether we even visit in the middle of current love affairs like a kind of halfway house, our Heartbreak Hotel awaits us. It will always wait to open and welcome us, just like another heart.

# GIVING UP ON
# GREATNESS

In high school I had three passions: gymnastics, the clarinet, and writing. I also had a grand plan—I'd support my play on the uneven bars and at the typewriter with a career as a first-chair concert clarinetist. My father was the first to point out to me that this scheme was akin to supporting one's starving by starving. Added to Father's strong disapproval was my unfortunate, though dazzling, leap into space during a northern Virginia gymnastic tournament, which ended my solo flights on the uneven bars.

Perhaps it was the fall from gymnastics that stunned me into my first artistic epiphany, but I prefer to think it was music itself. During our symphony's performance of a Mozart clarinet concerto, I was playing my third part with the happy abandon that always made my music teacher grimace slightly, her way of reminding me that excitement is not technique.

As Charles Donovan, our revered first-chair clarinetist,

163

moved eloquently into his solo, something strange happened to me: suddenly his music was moving through *my* body as if I, too, were no more than Charles's instrument. Charles's breath filled my lungs, his beautiful hands trembling against my own resting fingers. Utterly at this boy's command, I fell into a reverie akin to first love. But then I saw that he, too, was rapt, his body bowed beneath the authority of music in him.

I knew at that moment that *hearing* the music is not the same as simply listening. There was a difference between playing Mozart and letting Mozart play through me. I clearly saw that Charles's part was to reverberate with the perfect pitch of a tuning fork, a slim and human reed. It was this last understanding that for me stopped the music's flow. I realized: Charles Donovan was a genius, while I sat unworthily three rows away. I was only first chair, third clarinet—as far from the source of the sun as an undiscovered planet.

My chest caved in and I hunched over myself, clarinet in lap. I could not pick up my part. No matter. The others trooped along without me. For the next month after that performance, I canceled my clarinet lessons and played hooky from my seventh-period symphony. I betrayed music as I felt it had betrayed me—by *not* hearing it. Not from my sisters and brother on their French horn, oboe, and flute; not from my family's singing or my symphony mates involved in their earnest challenges climbing chair to chair. I even gave up writing my weekly mimeographed soap opera of the symphony, distributed like Russian samizdat among my friends. What was the point of all this artistic struggle if one wasn't as gifted as Charles?

At last I even gave up going to hear my high school symphony perform. How could I sit in an audience and not take my third chair? How listen and not hear my own clarinet part soaring distinct from the whole, from my hands? How could I remain still when my feet tapped out every rest and my fingers played or frayed the program, rolling it into a tiny paper clarinet? Then there were the faces of my friends in the symphony, familiar and yet transformed as the music pulsed through their bodies. There was not only the ecstasy of Charles Donovan but also my challenge partner, Lizzie Biskeborn, her eyes scanning the notes as if she followed them midflight; there was the first flautist with her silver woodwind trembling at her mouth with her most delicate kisses. There were one hundred upturned faces wide open and vulnerable as newborns, awaiting the conductor's baton to begin each movement, each breath. Then the music transfixed every player. They were private, yet as one in prayer and tribal worship.

The audience leaned toward the stage like plants toward light, mirroring back the meditation—all except me. I was out of sync, in shadow, separate, as ashamed and self-conscious as in that first Fall from grace. Somehow I'd lost myself—not in the music but in that narrow and never-ending labyrinth of my own criticism. After all, we were only a high school symphony; surely in New York or Boston or Salzburg Mozart was played perfectly, and in that stratosphere there was even someone more sublime than Charles. I clearly saw: we were young, we were country; we were just people, imperfectly pitched.

I was miserable in my mutiny. But I was also dimly aware that this retreat from music might be important, much the way I'd read about those yogis and priests leaving the world to better see and surrender to it. Was the act of abandoning something one loved a spiritual sacrifice, or was it the voice of the inner critic who whispered, "Why love so inadequately? Better to practice silence and self-restraint." Sadly, I catechized myself, most mystics never come back from their vows of silence, their holy, aloof caves. And that's how they save the world, if not themselves.

At the end of that school term, I resolved to sell my clarinet. A symphony friend was only too happy to buy it. I gave her the gleaming case, passing the beloved wooden Buffet to her as I might pass the main course to someone who still had an appetite. Expertly, she fit its lithe black lengths together. As she appreciatively held it up, I was struck by its familiar scent. It smelled like me—my hands, my own skin. This was startling, discovering my own essence in something I believed dead and beyond moving me.

"Please ..." I begged my friend, "don't *really* take it away from me." Then I burst into tears.

She was a second clarinetist, and kind. Without a word she put my clarinet back into its case and set it on my lap. I held it there for a long time without understanding anything. All I knew at that moment was that I had to play whatever instrument was mine, body and soul. I had to play because music was a way I would take in and give back to the world—it was the same as breathing.

And somehow I must have intuited then what I know now: It is the love of this world, moving through however imperfect a vehicle, however simple or small a gift, that makes us human, that makes us stay. For there is no leaving what we love.

Since that term when I abandoned my instrument, I've often reckoned with the fact that it may well be my fate in my art to be only first chair, third clarinet; that whatever passion I choose may not choose me. But if it's a choice between returning to that greater symphony or being forever lonely for a part of myself cast off simply because it is not a great gift, then let me keep my little chair, my worldly cave, three sections down from the Charles Donovans. And there let me always hear the holy music; let me play my imperfect part.

# III

# WAR DIARIES

# THE WAR THAT FELL TO EARTH

*January 16, 1991*

Last winter, during the Panama Invasion, our roof, which had always leaked, let loose a deluge in our living room. This is an old beach cottage braving Puget Sound's astonishing winds here at Alki Point, and my memories of Christmas 1989 are of watching the invasion on television accompanied by the pinging and dripping of rain into myriad buckets and metal bowls.

It was more than my roof and a far-off invasion that disturbed me. Our family feared that my little brother, a navy aviator, was in the fighting. We had not heard from him since he left on a mysterious top-secret mission the week before. We all waited for word. When my parents called, I could hardly hear the phone for the pounding of roof repairs. My brother was safe, at the Guantánamo Bay Naval Base, not in Panama after all. He was on standby and had not been ordered into the fray. Not this time.

My memories of Christmas are as secure as only a new

roof and a brother out of harm's way can assure. All that fell last year was the Berlin Wall, not house, sibling, or sky.

This Christmas week, as I sat, snowbound, watching yet another newscast of President Bush describing his single-minded plan to "kick ass," I noticed that the wind was picking up. Soon it had reached gale force and began ripping up trees along Alki by their one-hundred-year-old roots. When I drove around the point, spray from the twenty-foot waves hit my windshield and instantly froze. Amid all the calls from friends watching the news, my family rang.

"Looks like my squadron will be called up," my brother said softly. In our family, we always say the most horrible things in the tenderest tones. Two of my cousins are already in the Gulf, one a marine, the other a navy nurse-anesthesiologist. In this cousin's letters he explains why Bush called up the medical reserves first: "Once the hospital is ready, he can start the war." My cousin tells us this calmly, as if our president were an attending physician who is simply scheduling soldiers for surgery.

"Did you read Cousin Warren's last letter from the front?" my brother asked, excitement in his voice. It was electric, like an adrenaline rush. "The Iraqis have eaten half the animals in the Kuwaiti Zoo!"

I contemplated this as sixty-mile-an-hour winds battered my front windows and the front door banged on its old hinges. Somewhere halfway across the world there was a hospital waiting to be filled and a zoo that was half empty. What was this bloodthirst that had risen up these last two Christmases when we were supposed to be celebrating birth?

My father got on the other phone. "We're proud of

your brother," my father said. I felt that excitement again, in my father's voice; was this the sacrificial bliss of sending an only son off to war?

Long ago I remember my brother telling me that he had no memory of our father ever playing with him. I don't remember my father playing, period. An Ozark farm boy, he knew only work and war. We children described my father as "missing in action." If there was trouble at home—and there was plenty—it was a domestic matter, to be dealt with by the women's corps.

Our family was not the exception. With women then mostly at home and men of action in the field, is it any wonder that we now have a president who is also missing in any domestic action? Is it any coincidence that President Bush as the father of our country is acting the role of the man who ignores problems on the home front in order to pursue the manly issues abroad? Is this, perhaps, why he is not held accountable for leading us to the brink of a war no one wants simply because we are so familiar with the absent father that we no longer expect him to pay us any mind, even as our home collapses around us?

Is it contempt or fear or unfamiliarity with the domestic that makes our country's masculine embodiment so busy in far-off places? Is President Bush simply a mirror of the man who long ago abandoned his family or any attempt at putting his own country's house in order?

The day after my brother's call about his impending mobilization, I heard a terrible noise in the back of my house. At first I thought the pipes had frozen and exploded, as had the pipes of so many Seattle homes during our holiday on ice. But I saw to my despair that an entire section of my new roof was split open like so much skin and that the wind was operating there mercilessly. A vast graft of tar paper flew into the backyard, and then shingles began whirling around like leaden leaves.

I couldn't believe it. How could what was diligently fixed come unglued again? How could a new decade, begun in celebration and hope, find itself only one year later in disarray and disrepair?

I called the workman from last Christmas, defensive, ready to blast him if he refused to tend to a roof that before my eyes was tearing itself to pieces.

"We'll come right over," Doug, the owner of the construction company, said. "My roof work is always warranted. It's my responsibility."

I almost wept right there on the line. He didn't tell me to ignore what was broken in my house; he didn't show contempt for my small domestic problems by proclaiming that he was out fighting Evil with a foreign face that only he seemed to recognize. He didn't tell me that he'd attend to it later, after worse damage had been done. He didn't promise a peace dividend that never came.

*He* came. He and his stalwart crew of one man and one woman climbed atop that ravaged roof and patiently pounded it back in its proper place. It was nothing dramatic; as they worked the winds subsided, so they were not in any danger.

But I was excited. Not because I was at risk, but because I was safe. Being safe and keeping one's roof over one's head are two skills our country may have yet to learn in this new decade without enemies, when we perhaps learn at last to look inward, to come home to repair our own wounds, instead of making more. There is a heroism in what my workman did, and there is a vision that our country's leaders seem to have lost. Interestingly enough, my workman's company is called Vision Construction. I recommend that Doug and his crew take over my home front, since we have been so long abandoned.

# SAVING FACE

*March 27, 1991*

As a student, I once entered my college history-class to find this definition written on the black-board: "Intelligence is the ability to tolerate a high degree of ambiguity." It was twenty years ago, during the final years of the Vietnam War; my history project was a thesis on the World War II internment of Japanese-Americans in relocation camps—the dispossessed, the deeply suspected, and, for the duration of the war, the disappeared.

Between my interviews with the strangely polite and forgiving Nisei (second-generation Japanese-Americans) quietly rounded up for years of internment, I noticed that their children, many of them born in the camps, were the angry ones. It was as if the bitterness of silent defeat had gone inward, had been bred in the bones of the newborn. "Our parents never talk about intern-ment," a young camp-born Japanese-American told me.

"But they haven't forgotten how it felt to be prisoners in their own country."

Twenty years later I well remember how it felt sitting in a dark library carrel poring over periodicals from those war years. The way the Japanese were depicted in the news was chilling, revealing a racism I had seen strutting itself so blatantly in public only during my southern childhood, when the world was divided into black and white.

I'll never forget an article in *Time* magazine entitled "How to Tell Your Friends from the Japs." Two of the four portraits were of Chinese men, the other two Japanese. The accompanying discourse pointed out the difference between the "placid, kindly, open" expression of the Chinese and the "dogmatic, arrogant" expression of the Japanese. The Chinese are "relaxed, have an easy gait," while the Japanese "laugh loudly at the wrong time."

Two decades later, in the final days of another war—one that our government has gone to great trouble to distinguish from the anguish of Vietnam—I nevertheless saw the past repeated. I saw that divided face of war. On our side, I watched newscasts of American soldiers flashing V signs and boasting, "We own a piece of it!" deep in a desert that will never belong to us; I saw home-front celebrations with jukeboxes playing "We Are the Champions of the World"; I read an editorial by Tom Clancy in the *Los Angeles Times* crowing, "Does the US still have it? Ask the Iraqis." Finally, I saw shopping-mall models displaying the newest fad in clothing—the blood red, starry white, and night-sky blue of Old Glory waving on leather jackets, swimsuits, sweaters, and boxer shorts.

But what of the other face? What might an American face—the grinning GI, the fighter pilot with a thumbs-up sign as he heads off for a night of bombing Baghdad—look like to a vanquished people such as the Iraqis? An arrow points to the sharp-shooter eyes: "Does not see what damage he does." The close-cropped head: "Does not bow in sorrow, or humility." And finally, that cocksure smile: "Laughs loudly and at the wrong time."

As the estimated death toll for the Iraqis reaches a quarter of a million; as the danger of epidemic from bad water, no medicines, no sanitation, and little food threatens a country hitherto seen only as hostile, might we not temper our triumph with respect for the dead? Moving now into this limbo of postwar negotiations and subtle strategies, can we as Americans present another face to the world—one that is flexible, reflective, open to others who might not share our secure sense of strength?

"Justice is a fugitive from the camp of the victor," Homer wrote about another war millennia ago. To this one might add ambiguity as another fugitive. In all our history as a nation, America has never felt the shame of occupation, the crush and strut of triumphant armies trespassing against us, except in the Confederate South. I well remember a childhood of play wars in which the most unpopular kids were assigned the role of infidel Yankees. But most of our country has no memory of humiliating defeat.

It might be time to imagine the face and feelings of defeat, even as we rightfully celebrate the end of this desert war. In the midst of our laughter and reunions, we might remember the ravages of the Iraqi common people, who now live in a city bombed backward into another century, who must now tend to their souls, their families, their lives.

When asked to define growing up, my nine-year-old niece said simply, "Big people feel two things at the same time—that's why they never know whether to laugh or cry." That's how I feel. I keep seeing that divided face of the enemy and the friend. I keep remembering that my southern relatives still despise Yankees, that it was only in this past year, some fifty years after the fact, that Congress authorized reparations for those Japanese-Americans interned in American war camps during World War II. If one of our justifications for this war was stopping a worse, perhaps nuclear, Iraq of the future, we would do well to wonder what the children of Iraq will think of us as Americans as they grow up in a defeated homeland. Any peace in the future for our children and for the children of the Middle East will depend upon how we conduct ourselves in this postwar period, when ambiguity and reconciliation of seeming opposites will require all of our intelligence. Isn't it now time for us to show a face other than that of the victor?

If we can deepen our American character to embrace the humanity of the enemy, we might recognize that in the eyes of the world, Americans and Iraqis can both save our one very human face.

# ARMS AND THE MAN

*July 3, 1991*

I f no one listens," my grandfather said, his breath ragged, "I'll have to tell my story to a stranger." "Tell me, Grandpa," I whispered. Leaning closer to his hospital bed, I lightly touched his arm.

Inside his oxygen tent, he winced, then managed the suggestion of a grin. "Those Germans," he murmured with a grudging respect. "Never thought they'd lie in wait this long to ambush me." He gave me a rare direct gaze, his pale blue eyes so bright it hurt to look at him for long.

My maternal grandfather, eaten alive by pancreatic cancer, was not rambling. After many visits to his bedside, I was convinced that we were not in the hospital room but back in World War I with his unit, the army's Rainbow Division. My inheritance was a water-stained leather diary written in Grandfather's elegant hand. Here I kept up with caissons, war buddies, battles, death tolls, and the 1918 influenza outbreak on the home front, which killed more civilians than the war had American soldiers. This tiny white room teemed with the marching drama of the Great War.

"Oh, girlie," Grandfather said on that last visit. "I didn't write down the real story. I never told a living soul the truth. Strutting and singing and winning—that's all the women wanted to hear. And when I got back, well, no one likes a crybaby in the middle of a celebration, now do they?"

"Do you want to tell Uncle, too?"

"Not something you pass along to a son, sweet pea." He laughed and coughed and was not calm for a long time. "No," he said at last, exhausted. "I got to tell *them*." His eyes flickered around the room, meeting the eyes of the German soldiers who he believed had taken up residence in this close, antiseptic barracks. "And somebody still living."

He was quiet a long time. "You see, girlie, I killed them—not like you do these days with bombs and rockets—but with my bare hands. That one over there, I gutted him with my bayonet. His eyes rolled back in his head and he kept staring at me, like he wanted to see somebody's face while he was dying, even if it was his killer's. Never forget that look, no, I won't. Carried him with me like we were kin, like he was somebody to me instead of a stranger, another soldier.... Poor fellow on the wrong side of my gun like a stuck pig." Grandfather shivered, and I pulled the thin covers up over the feeding tubes in his belly. "Then there's that hefty fella, beet-faced still, don't you see, girlie? He got his head blown off and I found it in a field of cabbages looking like it just growed there. I didn't kill him, but I didn't bury him, either. I just kept grabbing those cabbages—that's all we lived on during that long march—first division to cross the Krauts' border, the first to see all the dead, theirs and ours." Suddenly my grandfather laughed. "You taking notes?" he demanded. His hand clawed mine and he said, "Don't call 'em Krauts when you tell my story to the family. No one can look at these faces so close now and call 'em Krauts. Besides, they're here to carry me on over. Ain't that a fine fiddle, girlie? I killed them and now they're gonna carry me."

I held his wasted hand, pocked with blue bruises from all the intravenous tubes and needles. His hand in mine felt like a cornhusk—light, with a faint vegetable rot. They say in the South that before a body dies it gives off the scent of crushed pumpkins. Grandpa smelled sweet and rank like compost.

"In the next war," my grandfather said, forcing himself to speak, his voice a rasping whisper, "think that fighter-pilot brother of yours will get haunted by those folks he bombs down below?"

"Don't know, Grandpa." It was 1976, and the aftermath of Vietnam was a long shadow falling between my Navy Reserve–captain father, my brother in boot camp training to be a navy aviator, and myself. Grandfather, once strongly in unison with the military element in my family, was now secretly deserting. Why was he passing his war stories down to me, instead of the men? If more fathers and grandfathers broke the war-hero taboo and told the real story, would it change anything?

This spring, in my dreams, I began to recall those last days when my grandfather again met the men he had killed. I was reminded of Grandpa's stories by the return from the Persian Gulf of my young cousin, a marine, whose unit was hit by friendly fire at Khafji.

My cousin Warren's letters home were filled with Bible verses and brave assurances that he was, at eighteen, ready to die for his country. When he returned from the Gulf last month, he was met by my parents and brother with proud backslaps and an invitation to speak before members of the CIA, my mother's employer. Instead, he asked to speak to my niece's third-grade class. The teachers and students eagerly awaited his tales of glory. But Warren's speech was brief, plainspoken.

"I saw too many John Wayne movies," he told the children. "I didn't know what war was until I saw two of my buddies blown up before my eyes—and they were killed by our own aircraft. I thought I wanted to be a lifer; now I want to be a schoolteacher. I don't want to ever go to war again." Warren's speech was not a big hit with the teachers or with most of the children. But there were a few who listened with grave faces, as if he were not just telling his story to strangers, as if our grandfather were now talking through him.

Stories help us look at what we do. My grandfather's final story was his deepest because he saw all points of view, poised as he was near his own death. The last time I saw him, he told me that two of the Germans had forgiven him, but there were so many more whom he needed to meet man to man. "You know, girlie"—my grandfather laughed—"that scripture, 'For now we see through a glass darkly, but then face to face'.... Well, I'm seeing face to face now. It's not judgment. It's more like meeting up with a man again I didn't much understand before. It's like meeting yourself coming and going, hah!"

Then he curled up within the translucent wings of his oxygen tent and sighed. "Sing to me, girlie."

Slowly I reached out and parted the plastic veil between us. Grandfather opened his eyes and nodded as I began the song he'd sung to me when I was small and had trouble breathing and curled around myself for comfort. "Over there, over there," I sang softly. "Send the word, send the word over there, say the Yanks are comin', the Yanks are comin', the Yanks are comin' so prepare...."

"*This* Yank is comin'," my grandfather breathed as if it were a prayer, as if all the others gathered around him in that room would hear how he came to take up arms, how he came now to be taken up in their arms.

# IV

# NATURE AND OTHER MOTHERS

# DOES AN EAGLE PLUCK OUT HER OWN EYES?—BEYOND THE TRAGIC VISION

When I first read Joseph Meeker's essays in *Wilderness* magazine, I was surprised to find that he belongs to the Northwest, sending his National Public Radio broadcasts, "Minding the Earth," off from Vashon Island. But after reading an earlier book, *The Comedy of Survival*, and his just-published *Minding the Earth* essay collection, I would think the Northwest proud to claim him. A writer of international and national repute, Meeker marries literature with ecology, to search for "the healthy compatibility of nature, mind, and art."

*The Comedy of Survival* is a truly original study of how our Western inheritance of the Greek tragic tradition has led us to the brink of ecological catastrophe. Meeker states, "Tragic writers, like engineers, have consistently chosen to affirm those values which regard the world as mankind's exclusive property." This penchant for celebrating tragedy pits man against nature—both his own

189

nature and Nature itself. In the Western tragic tradition, "personal greatness is achieved at the cost of great destruction." Tragic heroes are bent on transcending the natural order (and so life itself) to consciously choose their own moral order. We would not see, for example, a kingly eagle pluck out his own eyes as Oedipus does, to establish a moral universe. This inability to see nature past our own tragic projections prompts Meeker to suggest we put ourselves in truer perspective. "Spiritual and artistic creativity are not special powers provided so that humans can transcend the natural world," Meeker argues, "but features of human biological development useful for connecting humanity more deeply with the world."

Comedy or the picaresque tradition of not taking ourselves so seriously is what Meeker suggests might ensure our survival, as well as our Earth's. From *Hamlet* to Dante's *Divine Comedy*, Meeker's book is a profound romp through heretofore unexplored wilderness where our stories and our ecology meet and dance and teach.

Continuing in this comic tradition, *Minding the Earth* is a series of trim, eloquent essays with titles such as "People and Other Misused Resources," "Irony Deficiency," "Nurturing Chaos," and "Living Like a Glacier." Calling on his trainings as scientist, professor of literature, ecologist, and writer, Meeker's essays are gems of unexpected synthesis. For example, in "Bear Bearings," he tells us that before there was an Earth Mother, there was a Bear Mother. Great Goddess to our nomadic ancestors, the bear symbolized survival of winter and rebirth. That is why we use the phrase *to bear* children.

Among conservationists these days, there is hot

debate over exactly what our relationship to the Earth is. The seventeenth- and eighteenth-century man-against-nature attitude of early North and South American explorers or settlers, who stood vulnerable and all but lost in vast continents of primal forest, has given way to the less rapacious but perhaps equally antagonistic attitude of being keepers of the Earth. Federal agencies such as the Forest Service and the Bureau of Land Management have adopted this way of managing, or "multiple use" of the land. But this tradition is being challenged by such diverse movements as the radical environmentalism of Earth First!, the conservation lobbying tactics of groups like the Wilderness Society, and the more mystical, unifying vision of the Gaia hypothesis (in honor of the Earth Mother in Greek myth). This spring in San Diego the first scientific forum was held to debate this Gaia concept—that the Earth is a living, self-regulating organism.

Meeker's slant is that of human ecology, the interrelated study of human and natural processes. The essays here speak to this current debate by embracing scientific, spiritual, literary, and philosophical elements. In particular, "Assisi and the Steward," originally published in *Wilderness,* invoked the wrath of conservative Catholics and fundamentalists and brought fervent praise from some other Christians. The essay is sure to spark more controversy. Through it all Meeker takes a calm, scholarly tone to deftly delineate the differences between the world's major religions and their ecological beliefs. "In three of the five major religions" (Christianity, Judaism, Islam), "images of human power and authority are dominant and the main theme is stewardship," writes Meeker.

The original Old English word *stiweard* means "the warden of the sty ... pig-keeper." In its current environmental coinage a "steward" is one who manages God's property on God's behalf. These religions believe that humankind will be judged on how well it oversees this worldly Garden. The Hindu and Buddhist religions also see conservation as a "spiritual necessity," though they teach interdependence among all living things, including the Earth itself. To these religions, spirit is as much in a river or tree as in a human body, and "usefulness to humanity is not among the criteria for evaluating nature." We are in a debate, Meeker concludes, over "whether nature belongs to us, or we to it."

Whether he is tenderly chiding us to laugh a little more at our grand notions of tragic dominance or praising the trillium flower that shows us "it is possible to be beautiful while still retaining the benefits of uselessness," Meeker reminds us of our cosmic choice to connect with, rather than tragically transcend, our Earth.

# FISHING WITH FRIENDS

In early September, when the northwestern light was late and lulling, I went salmon fishing for the first time. My friend Flor Fernandez offered to share with me the subtle fisher's art—part pole, part tackle, part meditation—that her father had taught her in the dazzling azure waters off her native Cuba. Using fish bait of humble herring, sardines, and squid, they coaxed from blood-warm Caribbean waters red snapper, yellowtail, and barracuda.

Fishing here on Puget Sound, surrounded by Pacific ring-of-fire volcanic mountains, was a far sea gull's cry from Cuba. But as Flor calmly remarked, "Fishing is flexibility. You flow, you drift, you troll, you go in circles, you rock, you yield to the currents. Fishing is a feeling, no matter what country you're in. In fact," she added, "fishers are people without a country. They belong to whatever body of water supports them."

After ten years of living on the shores of Puget Sound,

I understand that I belong to this body of water. In the spring I set my ears to hear the bark of sea lions as an alarm clock; in the winter I watch for signs of a stray gray whale in midmigration. In the summer I take to the sound in a borrowed, battered wooden rowboat. But it had never occurred to me to fish there until that early autumn day when Flor arrived with her heavy-duty pole and a pound of frozen herring.

A net as big as another body lay between us in the boat. While Flor cut bait for a pole twice her height, I lay back with a smaller one, oars lazily dipping in the water. Around us other fishing skiffs broke out bag suppers, while the motorboats—one bedecked with a barbecue—cruised by with beer-can salutes. We floated in companionable reverie.

Suddenly, a pull from below. The pole was half out of my hands before I could begin to reel in the line. For several exhausting minutes I believed I'd snagged a sea monster; my arms were pliable as seaweed. Flor was no help. She had a big bite too and was wedging her feet against the boat to keep from being towed overboard. Then both lines went slack. We stared at each other, too breathless to speak.

"That," I finally got out, "was King Salmon."

Native Americans, I told Flor, say the first salmon is a visiting chief, and we must return him to the sea to make sure the Salmon People will keep coming back.

"But who can catch them?" Flor asked, stretching her sore muscles. "I'd starve to death if salmon were the only fish in these waters."

We did hook a rock cod and a sun perch. Though we got other mighty bites, it was obvious we weren't fishing for the wily salmon, we were feeding them. The sun tilted over the Olympics, and I rowed us home.

As I leaned wearily into the oars my ears pricked to underwater sounds, high-pitched squeals and clicks I half recognized before the water erupted into bubbles around our boat and we began to spin in a slow whirlpool.

"Orcas!" I shouted. "Everywhere!" I leaned over, plunging my hands into the roiling bubbles.

"We'll capsize!" Flor yelled.

I assured her that orcas don't attack humans, but Flor looked doubtful as our boat was sucked into the closing bubble net that herding orcas breathe to round up fish. Any minute a killer whale might have breached to feed, great toothed mouth gaping. I started singing at the top of my lungs (I'd heard that orcas, who have their own complicated language, respond to our music). As we swirled around in this eerie, churning eye, I heard a yelp. Flor had something on her line.

She effortlessly pulled in a shining coho salmon. At that moment the orcas kindly set us free. Black-and-white bodies slipped below, then surfaced far off with a *whoosh*, in search of other fishing grounds.

"It's the first salmon," Flor said. "The orcas caught it for us."

In the pale twilight she held up the elegant fish, its silvery scales glinting with their own light. Without a word she gently unhooked the salmon; it arched and dove back into the sound. We rowed toward shore, assured that the Salmon People would return.

# THE WATER WAY

If landscape is character, then northwesterners are most like water. We are shaped by the voluptuous shores and salt tides of Puget Sound, the deep currents of the Columbia, Salmon, and Snake rivers; finally, we are held back from falling off the proverbial edge of the world by a Pacific coastline whose nurturing rain forests and rocky peninsulas face the sea like guardians. So surrounded by water, we cannot impose our own rhythms on nature as easily as a bulldozer does on a southern California canyon. It is we who find ourselves subtly in sync with the rise and fall of tides, the ebb and flow of the natural world.

This distinction—that northwesterners are more changed by their environment than it is by us—is crucial to understanding our character. Recently, a convention of New Yorkers visited Seattle. On the harbor cruise to Blake Island, birthplace of Chief Sealth (Seattle) for a salmon feast hosted by Native Americans to re-create the first salmon bake and potlatch ceremonies that defined tribal life here for thousands of years, the tourists commented that everything seemed in slow motion.

"We've had to shift gears," said one New Yorker, somewhat anxiously. "Everything's so laid back. Maybe it's all those negative ions in the atmosphere."

Another visitor said, "How do you stand traffic jams on those floating bridges. Can't they just pave a part of Lake Washington?"

Finally, a rather pensive, bespectacled literary agent remarked, "Now I know why Seattle is singlehandedly keeping New York's book business alive. You have to go inside in all this gray and wet. I feel like I'm dreaming."

"Must be why Seattle has espresso carts on every corner and some of the world's best coffee." Someone laughed. "It's to keep yourselves awake!"

Northwesterners are a dreamy lot. We're in a fine tradition of dreamers. According to the Wasco Indians along the Columbia River, the tribe knew long before the white people came to settle at Alki Point, in 1851, that a change was coming. As told in Ella E. Clark's classic *Indian Legends of the Pacific Northwest,* one of the Wasco elders dreamed that "white people with hair on their faces will come from the rising sun." The strangers were prophesied to bring with them "iron birds that could fly" and "something—if you just point it at anything moving, that thing will fall down and die." They also brought new tools such as axes, hatchets, and stoves. Along with this new technology, the white people brought a philosophy of individual ownership of the land.

The Native Americans knew that the land could never be owned, just as it was impossible to section off the vast winding lengths of the emerald-clear body of Puget Sound, so like a watery dragon embracing the land. Even now, after over a century of non-Indian dominance, Puget Sound property rights ebb and flow according to the tides, not the set boundaries of so-called landowners. If even our ownership of northwest land is called into daily question by changing tides, how much more deeply are we affected by water?

Physicists posit that by observing something, we subtly change it; does what we deeply gaze upon, then, also change us? Northwesterners not only reckon with water shaping our physical boundaries, we must also learn to live most of the year as if underwater. Rain is a northwest native. Our famous rainfall is perhaps all that shelters us from the massive population and industrial exploitations of nearby California. The rain is so omnipresent, especially between late October and even into June, that most northwesterners disdain umbrellas, the true sign of any tourist.

Widely acclaimed Port Angeles poet Tess Gallagher tells it this way, "It is a faithful rain. You feel it has some allegiance to the trees and the people.... It brings an ongoing thoughtfulness to their faces, a meditativeness that causes them to fall silent for long periods, to stand at their windows looking out at nothing in particular. The people walk in the rain as within some spirit they wish not to offend with resistance."

One must be rather fluid to live underwater; one must learn to flow with a pulse greater than one's own. A tolerance for misting gray days means an acceptance that life itself is not black and white, but in between. If the horizons outside one's window are not sharply defined but

ease into a sky intimately merged with sea and soft landscape, then perhaps shadows, both personal and collective, are not so terrifying. After all, most of the year
northwesterners can't even see their own literal shadows
cast on the ground. We live inside the rain shadow. We
tolerate edges and differences in people and places perhaps because our landscape blends and blurs as it
embraces.

There is a strong Asian influence here in the Pacific
Northwest. Seattle's expansive harbor is a gateway to the
Orient, and the strong, graceful pull of that more feminine culture is felt here. In fact, the classic *Tao Te Ching*
by the ancient Chinese master Lao-tzu, could well have
described the Puget Sound landscape and character:

> Nothing in the world
> is as soft and yielding as water.
> Yet for dissolving the hard and inflexible,
> nothing can surpass it.
>
> The soft overcomes the hard;
> the gentle overcomes the rigid.

Our northwest character is flexible, fluid. There are
not the rigid social strata of New England or the South.
There are not the climatic extremes that make for a siz-
zling summer race riot in Watts or the violent cold of
Chicago. Even the first Native Americans were known not
as warriors so much as fishermen. While there were territory battles, there was also a diversity and abundance of
food that made quite a different story from the southwest
tribal struggles over scarce resources. Amidst this plenti-

tude, northwest art flourished—so did storytelling.

In keeping with the landscape's watery changes, the northwest Native stories are full of legends in which animals change easily into people and back again. For example, the Salmon People are an underwater tribe who also spend a season on land; the whales and seals can metamorphose into humans as easily as the ever-present mist and clouds change shape. Many northwest coast tribes tell of merpeople, part human, part mammal, who mediate between the worlds to keep a watery balance. One of the most common gods was called "Changer." Many Native tribes began their mythologies with water—floods and seas creating what we now call "the people." A Skagit myth details this beginning, when Changer decided "to make all the rivers flow only one way" and that "there should be bends in the rivers, so that there would be eddies where the fish could stop and rest. Changer decided that beasts should be placed in the forests. Human beings would have to keep out of their way."

Here in the Northwest it is we humans, not water, who must keep out of the way. We pride ourselves on living within nature's watery laws, on listening to our environment before it is irreparably lost and silenced. It is, after all, here in the Northwest where the last nurturing old-growth forests still stand, where people fight fiercely to preserve them for future generations. Here is also where the country's last salmon still spawn. But for all their strong conservation of nature, there are signs that even the "Rainy-Day People" are facing growing environmental challenges.

Oil spills blacken our beaches, and several species of salmon are endangered; gray whales are found on their migrating courses belly-up from pollution in Puget Sound. There have been major closures of shellfish beds throughout the region because of toxic contaminations from industrial waste. And, as always, the old-growth forest debate rages between loggers and those who struggle to conserve the trees.

The Puget Sound Alliance, a local program to protect Puget Sound, employs a full-time soundkeeper, who patrols the shores checking reports of pollution. There is the highly acclaimed whale museum and its staff in Friday Harbor, who have been studying the transient and resident pods of orcas in the San Juans for many years. Greenpeace is highly visible in the Northwest, as are local grass-roots organizations formed to save well-loved forests and wetlands. There is a growing movement among corporations whose headquarters are in the West to give back some of their profits to protect our wilderness—REI and Patagonia are two such businesses who believe in investing in their own region's environmental resources. Such bioregionalism runs strong in the Northwest. After all, many people moved here to be closer to the natural world. The urban sprawl of California, the East Coast penchant for putting nature in last place—this is the mind-set most northwesterners sought to escape and seek to guard against.

Just as northwesterners claim closeness with their natural world, so too we are close to our own history. Compared with the Native tribes, we are young. Our history here is only 150-odd years, compared with thousands of years of Skagit, Suquamish, Muckleshoot, Okanogan, and multitudinous other tribal roots. Some of these Indian myths calmly predict that "the human beings will not live on this Earth forever." This is an agreement between Raven, Mink, Coyote, and what the Skagits call "Old Creator." The prophecy predicts that human beings "will stay only for a short time. Then the body will go back to the Earth and the spirit back to the spirit world." The possibility of this simple ebb and flow of our human tribe seems more resonant here—here where the animals interchange lives with the humans, where the mists can transform entire settlements and skyscrapers into low-hung cloud banks.

Our human conceits carry less weight in this watery world. Perhaps this is why during the first days of the Persian Gulf War, as during those seventy-two hours of the failed coup in the Soviet Union, it was remarked that there were more fishing boats on Puget Sound than usual. It is typically northwestern that this gone-fishing-while-the-world-falls-apart attitude prevails while in other areas of the country the population is transfixed by CNN. It is not that northwesterners aren't deeply involved, it's just that nature can be an antidote to such strong doses of terror. Nature can also remind us that there are other mysteries at work in the world, which might hold more power than our own. And more hope. Li Po, ancient Taoist sage, writes:

Since water still flows, though we cut it with swords
And sorrow returns, though we drown it with wine,
Since the world can in no way answer to our craving,
I will loosen my hair tomorrow and take to a fishingboat.

If water is our northwest character and rainy reverie our temperament, it follows that those of us who stay long in the Pacific Northwest must develop an inner life to sustain us through the flow of so many changing gray days. This means that ambition is not only an outward thrust toward manipulating our environment; ambition may also be an inner journey, not to change but to understand the often unexplored territory within, what Rilke calls "the dark light." Are we a more mystical region and people? Let's just say the climate is there and so is the water way.

# PRACTICING FOR
# ANOTHER COMMUTE

I first arrived in Seattle during a New Year's blizzard, and I lived a month on Mercer Island without once seeing Mount Rainier. It was mid-February when I got my first glimpse of that mythical mountain—and it was almost the last thing I saw.

My friend B.J. and I were driving across the sturdy, low-in-the-water bridge one midwinter morning. It was a glorious day, sun startling away those Seattle mists, which I knew hid a mountain that awed local folks like some fabled Isle of Avalon. But having myself lived high in the Rockies, I privately thought it somewhat amusing that so much was made in this city about hills and *one* mountain.

I was not prepared that morning to glance from oncoming bridge traffic to the lake and see a dazzling white whale breeching way up out of the waves—over the guardrail, breathing in the bridge, the whole horizon, all the air. I gasped and let go the steering wheel, turning to meet that mountain full face. It wasn't faith or terror that made my whole body turn toward Mount Rainier; it was more instinctive, like the way something vegetable in us faces the sun.

My car swerved, tires thump-thumping against the cement guard curb, then bouncing back to dart into the dangerous reversible lane.

"You never get used to it," B.J. said calmly, reaching across and righting the steering wheel as simply as if we'd been playing bumper cars. "Not really. We just pretend it doesn't overwhelm us."

She was smiling, nodding to Mount Rainier as casually as if bidding howdy-do to a big, a really big, neighbor. But to me that day when I lost control of my car, my caution, my grown-up and carefully contained capacity for awe, it was as if I'd seen the sky split open to reveal that god or goddess the child in me always believed lived in clouds.

For a year I commuted across the bridge; from my study at night I stared at the floating globes of white, the red zip of taillights, the bright, oncoming eyes of cars streaking across a dark expanse. Since the mountain was so rarely around, it was the bridge I memorized, in the way that we will commit to memory a certain road, or room, or smell that suggests a lover, a leave-taking, a life's change.

The Mercer Island Floating Bridge became for me that year a daily ritual, a kind of meditation, a movement between parts of myself. I dreamed about the bridge, made it my own, and so it became important in my life in a way I was not to understand fully until the end of that year and my time on Mercer Island.

That year my friend B.J. died on Mercer Island. Death, like Mount Rainier, is a thing we never really get used to. As I was driving back across the bridge that day of B.J.'s death, the mountain was obscured by mists, but I saw and felt something just as amazing as Mount Rainier. I saw the faces of all those commuters—face after face after face coming toward me in waves.

And where before those faces had seemed wrapped in their own mists, unknowable, now their humanity was no longer hidden. I caught my breath. How brave, how frail, how naked the faces seemed in that after-death aura B.J.'s passing left me. In those brief, passing faces I saw a beauty and vulnerability that broke my heart. Did they know they were mortal? Did all these commuters know that they might leave in the morning and never return—or return to find the fabric of their lives rent wide? How do we keep driving every day across this Mercer Island Bridge knowing how fragile the link is?

I started shaking, hands on the steering wheel just like that day when I'd first seen Mount Rainier. I turned in its direction, looking for its massive, assuring solidness like a sign, something to steady me. Then I remembered B.J. saying that we had to pretend the mountain didn't overwhelm us, as life does from time to time.

So I looked instead at all those faces, the brave and the sad and the wondrous and the weary who commute between life and death while a great mountain silently witnesses. And I finally felt what steadied my hands on the wheel: I felt the presence, though invisible, of that dispassionate mountain; I felt the stretch of the steel bridge like courage, like a human umbilical between what we know and what we believe.

Now when I commute across the Mercer Island Floating Bridge, I consider it practice for another commute. I keep my hands steady on the wheel, my car surely on the bridge—even when sometimes the sky splits open and, small as I am, I see something so much larger.

# KILLING OUR ELDERS

As a small child growing up on a Forest Service lookout station in the High Sierras near the Oregon border, I believed the encircling tribe of trees were silent neighbors who protectively held the sky up over our rough cabins. The Standing People, I'd heard them called—but that was later, when I could almost understand the rapid-fire noises people aimed toward one another like so much scattershot. Because the trees were taller and older than grown-ups, and because all of us—from snake to squirrel to people—were obviously related, I assumed that the trees were our ancestors. After all, they were here before us. So we were their children.

For all their soaring, deep stillness, the ponderosa pines and giant Douglas firs often made noises in the night, a language of whispers and soft whistles that sang through the cabin's lying-down walls of their pine kinfolk like a woodwind lullaby. I first memorized the forest with my hands, crawling on all fours across prickly pine needles. Like a blind girl's reading braille, my stubby fingers traced sworls of pine bark, searching for congealed sap. I'd chew its fragrant pine gum—more flavorful than any bland baby food. The snap of pine sap against my tongue woke up my nose, face, and brain; I'd wriggle my face in delight, which earned me the nickname Gopher.

Toddlers didn't have to be human yet up there in the forest. Adults called us animal or vegetable names like Coon or Pumpkin Head or Skunk. And the trees didn't have to be not-alive, or dead timber. Forty years ago, when I was born on that Pacific Northwest forest, the old trees still stood in abundance. Clear-cutting hadn't yet become official policy. Forty years ago, my ancestors still stood watch over me, over us all.

Late last August a friend and I drove through those High Sierra and Cascade forests again on a road trip from Los Angeles to my home in Seattle. In the four-hour drive between the old mining town of Yreka in northern California and Eugene, Oregon, we counted fifty logging trucks, roughly one every four minutes. Many of the flatbeds were loaded with only one or two huge trees. I don't know when I started crying, whether it was the crazy-quilt scars of clear-cutting or the sullen bumper sticker in Drain, Oregon, heart of logging country, that read: WHEN YOU'RE OUT OF TOILET PAPER, USE A SPOTTED OWL! Maybe it was when we called our friend's cabin on Oregon's Snake River, outside of Merced, and he told us that every day, from dawn to dark, a logging truck had lumbered by every five minutes. "It's like a funeral procession out of the forest," my friend Joe said. "It's panic logging; they're running shifts night and day before the winter or the Congress closes in on them."

As I drove through those once lush mountains, I noticed my fingers went angry-white from clenching the steering wheel every time a logging truck literally lumbered by me. I wondered about the loggers. They, too, grew up in the forest; their small hands also learned that bark is another kind of skin. Among these generations of logging families, there is a symbiotic love for the trees. Why then this desperate slashing of their own old-growth elders? Is it simply, as Oscar Wilde wrote, the way we humans love?

> Yet each man kills the thing he loves ...
> The coward does it with a kiss,
> The brave man with a sword!

Or a chain saw.

But it's too easy to blame the loggers and timber companies for the past decade's destruction of over 90 percent of our old-growth forests. Aren't those armies of logging trucks simply following orders our national need has given them?

Amidst all the politics of timber and conservation, there is something sorely missing. Who are the trees to us? What is our connection to them on a deeper level than product? In the 500,000 years of human history throughout Old Europe, the pagans worshiped trees. The word *pagan* means simply "of the land." When we recognized that our fate was directly linked to the land, trees were holy. Cutting down a sacred oak, for example, meant the severest punishment: the offender was gutted at the navel, his intestines wrapped around the tree stump so tree and man died together.

Our pagan ancestors believed that trees were more important than people, because the old forests survived and contributed to the whole for many more than one human lifetime. Between 4,000 and 5,000 years ago in our own country once stood the giant sequoias in the Sierra Nevadas. Most of these great trees are gone; but in Sequoia National Park there is the General Sherman Tree. Thousands pay homage to it every year. And no wonder. According to Chris Maser in *Forest Primeval: The Natural History of an Ancient Forest,* the General Sherman Tree "was estimated to be 3,800 years old in 1968. It would have germinated in 1832 B.C. ...[it] would have been 632 years old when the Trojan War was fought in 1200 B.C. and 1,056 years old when the first Olympic Games were held in 776 B.C. It would have been 1,617 years old when the Great Wall of China was built in 215 B.C. and 1,832 years old when Jesus was born in Bethlehem."

How have we come to lose our awe and reverence for these old trees? Why have we put our short-term needs for two or three generations of jobs before our respect for our own past and our future? As we drove past the Pacific Northwest sawmills, I was startled to see stockpiled logs, enough for two or three years of processing. And still the logging trucks thundered up and down the mountain roads.

To quiet my own rising panic over such a timber rampage, I tried to understand: "What if trees were people," I asked myself. "Would we treat them differently?" My initial response was "Well, if old trees were old people, of course, we'd preserve them, for their wisdom, their stories, the history they hold of us." But with a shock I realized that the reason we can slash our old-growth forests is the same reason we deny our own human elders a place in our tribe. If an old tree, like our old people, is not perceived as *productive*, it might as well be dead.

Two years ago this winter, my grandfather died. An Ozarkian hard-times farmer and ex-sheriff, Grandaddy was larger than life to the gaggle of grandchildren who gathered at his farm almost every summer vacation. Speaking in a dialect so deep it would need subtitles today, he'd rail against the "blaggarts" (blackguards) and "scoundrills" (scoundrels) he sought to jail for every crime from moonshining to murder. One of my earliest memories is playing checkers with a minor scoundrel in Grandaddy's jail. Another is of bouncing in the back of his pickup as he campaigned for reelection, honking his horn at every speakeasy and shouting out, "I'll shut ya down, I will, quicker 'n Christ comin' like a thief in the night!" I also remember Grandaddy sobbing his eyes out over his old hound's death. "It's just that he won't never be alongside me no more," Grandaddy explained to us. Somebody gave him a young hound pup, but Grandad was offended. "You can't replace all that knowin' of an old hound with this pup. That hound, he took care of me. Now, I gotta take care of this young'un."

My grandaddy's funeral was the first time I'd ever seen all my kinfolk cry together. Without reserve, some thirty-odd people in a small backwoods church sobbed—bodies bent double, their breathing ragged. It was a grief distinct from the despair I'd heard at the deaths of an infant or a contemporary. At my grandaddy's funeral, we all, no matter what age, cried like lost children. We were not so much sad as lonely. We were not so much bereft as abandoned. Who would tell us stories of our people? Who would offer us the wisdom of the longtime survivor? Our grandfather, this most beloved elder, was no longer alongside us.

When I returned home from the funeral, someone asked me, "How old was he?" When I replied eighty-six, this person visibly lightened. He actually made a small shrug of his shoulders. "Oh, well, then ..." He dismissed the death as if it were less a loss than if it had been of a person in his prime. I wondered if the man might next suggest that I get myself a new hound puppy.

The nowadays notion that people, like parts, are replaceable and that old parts are meant to be cast aside for newer models is a direct result of an industrial age that sees the body and the Earth as machines. In the preindustrial, pagan or agrarian society, the death of an elder was cause for great sorrow and ceremony. In our modern-day arrogance, we equate numbers with value.

If, for example, my grandaddy were one of those old Douglas firs I saw in the forest funeral procession, would he really be equaled by a tiny sapling? Old trees like old people survive the ravages of middle-age competition for light or limelight; they give back to their generations more oxygen, more stories; they are tall and farsighted enough to see the future because they are so firmly rooted in the past. Old growth, whether tree or person, give nurturing; the young saplings planted supposedly to replace them *need* nurturing.

As a nation are we still so young, do we still worship what is newborn or newly invented so much that we will be eternal adolescents, rebelling against the old order of trees or people? If our 200-year-old country were a 200-year-old Douglas fir, would we see ourselves as no more than prime timber to cut down and sell to Japan? Maturity teaches us limits and respect for those limits within and around us. This means limiting perhaps our needs, seeing the forest for the timber. If we keep sending all our old trees to the sawmills to die, if we keep shunting off our elders to nursing homes to die, if we keep denying death by believing we can replace it with what's new, we will not only have no past left us, we will have no future.

A Nez Percé Indian woman from Oregon recently told me that in her tradition there was a time when the ancient trees were living burial tombs for her people. Upon the death of a tribal elder, a great tree was scooped out enough to hold the folded, fetuslike body. Then the bark was laid back to grow over the small bones like a rough-hewn skin graft.

"The old trees held our old people for thousands of years," she said softly. "If you cut those ancient trees, you lose all your own ancestors, everyone who came before you. Such loneliness is unbearable."

Aren't we all in a way native Americans now? Can we at last recognize that we are one tribe, one forest, that the last standing old trees in our country are crucial to our well-being, our own long-term growth? Here in the Pacific Northwest, where the loggers are slashing their way to a last stand, where the environmentalists are pounding nails in old growth to thwart the chain saws—as if the trees were again a crucifixion cross—here we might stop ourselves in time to recognize that both old-growth trees and old-growth people are sacred.

"We can only heal so much," writes Deena Metzger in her poem "The Buddha of the Beasts." "The thousand year old trees will not return in the lifetime of my species."

I will always be lonely for my grandfather; the child in me will always long for my first tribe of Standing People who watched over me. On some spiritual level, our human entrails are still wrapped around the trees, like an umbilical cord. And every time a great tree is cut, our kind die too—lonely and longing for what we may some-day recognize as ourselves.

Of all my family's elders, I now have only one blood-kin grandparent left. Grandmother Elsie May is ninety-six years old and though she has acute leukemia, her mem-ory still astonishes us. A farm girl from Southern Mis-souri, who once taught astronomy to college students, my grandmother has made it her life's passion to know birds the way she once memorized stars. She calls them by name, she knows their nests and their migrations, she whistles harmonies with her favorite songbird, the blaz-ing cardinal. "Birds belong to both worlds, earth and sky," she taught us. "So do trees, so do people."

I will always call upon my Standing People and grand-parents, all my elders, to remind me that if I remember I am not simply human but also tree and bird and mam-mal, I will never be lonely—I will belong.